EAGLE'S TALON GRAY

S. J. Reisner

EAGLE'S TALON GRAY

Sorcerers' Twilight Book Three

S. J. Reisner

Darkerwood Publishing Group
United States of America

S. J. Reaisner   Eagle's Talon Gray, Sorcerers' Twilight Book Three

Darkerwood Publishing Group, Arvada, CO
ISBN 978-1-938839-08-5

Cover Art © 2016 by Ermisenda Alvarez
Editorial – W. Briar

darkerwoodpublishing.com

Sorcerers' Twilight Books:

Left Horse Black (Book One)

Warrior's Blood Red (Book Two)

Eagle's Talon Gray (Book Three)

Other Books by S. J. Reisner

Saving Sarah May

The Unicorns War Softly

Grendel's Dragon

ACKNOWLEDGEMENTS

Left Horse Black and the entire *Sorcerers' Twilight* trilogy was a journey I began back in 1992. As a young, bright-eyed writer at the tender age of nineteen, I had big dreams and high hopes. That first book was initially 3-4 different books that became *Left Horse Black* after thirteen long years. In my early years, I was deeply inspired by the late David Eddings, whose Belgariad and Malloreon series I devoured between classes in the quad at Metropolitan State University in Denver.

I started this series as a reader and an aspiring novelist, not really knowing how to craft a story. While I still have my shortcomings as an author, I have come to realize that this series was a journey for me. It was a test in finishing what I started. The first book brought me my first publishing contract, and it was also the first novel I self-published after the initial publishing contract went sour. More importantly, this series shows my growth as a writer from the very first chapter I turned in for a creative writing workshop back in 1992, to the last edited chapter at the end of this book in 2018. It was through this series that I discovered my voice, tested my perseverance, and challenged myself.

All books need acknowledgements because so many people are involved in bringing each one to publication. First and foremost, for this book, a huge thank you goes out to my editor, Will, who without, *Eagle's Talon Gray* would not have been nearly as cohesive and polished. It has been hard bringing this series to a close and Will helped me with that. I think subconsciously I never wanted Tnasha's journey to end.

Next - a huge thank you to my mom and sister who always encouraged me to keep working on *Sorcerers' Twilight* to the end. A thankful bow goes to Ermisenda Alvarez, my cover artist, who updated the covers to their current incarnation (and did a fabulous job). A thank you to Shaelyn, for being a fabulous first reader.

Heartfelt thanks also go out to my all my RMFW IPAL friends, but specifically Lisa, for her introduction of NovelRama, and to Corinne for helping me to get organized and get things done! You both inspired me and, in your own way, helped me finish this novel and this series.

Thank you to my first critique groups for making me feel insecure and unsure of myself and making me feel like I sucked and was wasting my time on a series that was going nowhere. While Sorcerers' Twilight is certainly not the Belgariad and I'm no David Eddings, I am S. J. Reisner and this story is uniquely me. You helped me come to peace with that.

Finally, a huge thank you to my beta readers and those readers who read everything I pen. You all keep me going.

DEDICATION

For my dedicated readers and supporters. Thank you for your patience and encouragement over the years.

The West Ocean Mainlands

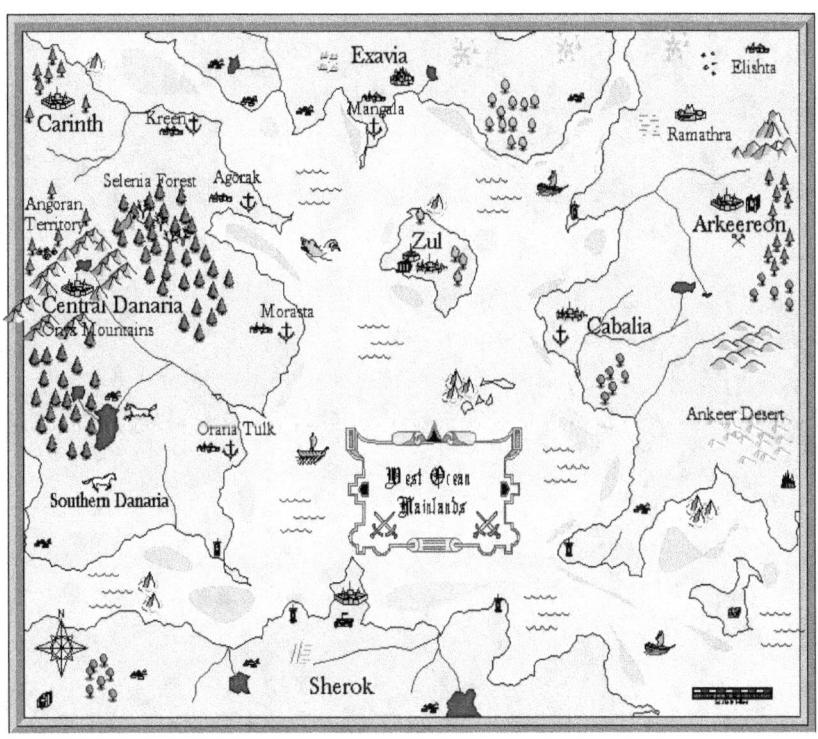

Chapter 1

The physician pulled Priestess Caitlan aside. "We must try other measures. Our current treatment of her condition isn't working."

The man looked unusually pale and gaunt in the dim room. Caitlan couldn't help but let out a sigh.

"Mage-blood is a fickle thing, medically speaking, of course," he said.

Caitlan's normally cheerful attitude had all but diminished in the past month. She took a deep breath and held back the tears she felt surfacing in the corners of her eyes. "The seeress, Amy, has an idea. She cannot visit as often, but she and Priestess Shanalyn believe that moving Tnasha's arms and legs for her might force her mana to begin circulating again."

"At this juncture I believe we should try everything." With a sad smile, the physician opened the door and beckoned her through it. "Perhaps we should let her be for awhile. There's nothing more to be done now."

Tnasha heard their voices and heard the door close as they left the room. Caught in a mana paralysis, she opened her eyes and strained to see all she could. She could not speak, but she could hear her own breath, and feel her chest rise and fall with every measured inhale and exhale. The staff, the Eagle's Talon, stood propped against the wall in front of her bed. It appeared unremarkable sitting there and to an untrained eye, looked nothing like the powerful weapon it could be in the wrong hands. Every time Tnasha looked at the staff, a tinge of sadness overwhelmed her. Not that it reminded her of better days, but rather it reminded her of him. Lord Aithian. At the time, he had been a trusted friend trying to help her save the world from the Kersian Sorcerer Seth's plan to become an overlord. But now, across the ocean with time and distance between them, she wondered if she felt something more for Aithian. She cursed herself for not paying more attention. Did he think of her?

She groaned inwardly, mindfully chastising herself for her ridiculous thinking. After all, she wasn't some naive girl pining for love and marriage. She was a focused soldier and sorceress who, when given a task, pursued it tirelessly without complaint. She felt her lids growing heavy. Images of her time in the Kersian stronghold and the brave Arkeeronish sorcerers who had helped her began to diminish. The final image was of Aithian's strong jaw, tawny skin, and dark hair fading into nothing. She sighed, wondering then if she was selfish for only thinking of herself. At least she had time to think. The mana paralysis, brought on by extensive overuse of sorcery, had given her that. From morning until night, she watched as the world went on without her.

Occasionally the Seeress Amy would visit and they could speak to one another with telepathy. Not all sorcerers could project thoughts. Luckily, Amy was adept, and Tnasha learned quickly. It was how the physician and other sorcerers knew that Tnasha was quite active mentally, despite her poor physical condition. She looked forward to Amy's visits, but Amy only came every other day. Between those few hours of having someone to talk to, she lay helpless and trapped in her own thoughts. Her body, every muscle and nerve, remained frozen, or so it seemed. The beautiful sheen of violet mana that emanated from her body, that should have been fluid and always active, now stood stolid and unmoving.

No one knew if her mana would begin moving again, or if the paralysis would eventually lead to atrophy and then death. High Priestess Caitlan of the Temple Dagon brought her carefully crafted medicinal teas flavored with hibiscus and honey in hopes Tnasha would gather some nourishment from them. Tnasha needed help to drink the teas, but she enjoyed their bitter sweet taste. Tnasha did not feel the pangs of hunger, nor did she feel weak unless her body was on the verge of its regular sleep cycle as it was now. She simply could not move. Tea after tea, nothing seemed to work, and Caitlan's patience wore thin. Tnasha could sense the Priestess' resignation with each deep sigh that escaped her. Even then, Caitlan would force a reassuring smile. So, every day, several cups of tea were poured down her throat.

Tnasha went over it again in her head as if reliving what had happened would somehow keep her alive despite her body's best effort to betray her. The Sorcerer Morvack raced against her to Arkeereon to gain the magical weapon harbored there in the frozen wasteland of Ramathra. His brother, Seth, a brutal warrior who killed for pleasure, followed and beat them to the weapon. One mana blate directed through the stone of the Raven's Claw had knocked Tnasha, her companions, and even Morvack into unconsciousness. While the journey back to Arkeereon was somewhat foggy in her memory, she remembered Arkeereon itself well. The mood amongst those in its hierarchy left the halls of their fortress bleak. Arkeereon was nothing like Danaria, where sorcerers were not confined behind thick walls of brick and mortar.

Their isolation, however, was voluntary. Knowing the sorcerer bloodlines were dying, even their own, the Arkeeronish seemed resigned to their fate. Realizing he no longer had a place in Seth's plan to rule the world, Morvack had stayed in Arkeereon where he was welcomed. His own blood could help the hierarchy extend their bloodline another generation. Even then, there were many sorcerers and few sorceresses. Their dismal numbers left them helpless to an uncertain fate, a fate that Danaria faced as well. The only sorcerer faction that seemed to have any hope were the Angoran's, but even their bloodlines had thinned over the years.

Tnasha let out a sigh and thought back to Zul. There, they had been successful in taking care of Gavgal's brothers Seth and Alax. Seth's final blate had hit her even though she tried to block it. It was Seth's fault she was paralyzed. Each time she remembered this, her anger grew. She closed her eyes then, trying to force her mana to move. If her mentor, Kalath, were still alive, he could have helped her. Healed her. But Seth killed Kalath as well. What would Kalath tell her to do?

He would tell me to visualize the mana moving, and when it didn't work, he'd tell me I wasn't trying hard enough, she thought. She imagined her mana moving and fluid, like a river of violet circling her body in tendrils of light. It was no use. It remained firm and still. A tear of frustration escaped the corner of her eye. *Lord Liale,* she prayed to the Earth element silently, *why have you allowed this to happen to me?* The anger ripped her up inside. Trying to find any excuse for her predicament, she decided to blame her weakness on the daily ritual to the god *Liale,* that she had hastily given up earlier in her training. How could she have been so foolish to believe that her strength came from within? Pride be damned. Exhausted from arguing with herself, Tnasha's mind collapsed in on itself and she fell headlong into a dream.

The horses were charging again. She stood on a cliff, overlooking a deep blue ocean. The water below crashed onto the jagged rocks. Even asleep, she remembered this dream from dreams past. She turned around expecting to see the Kersians with Morvack leading their hordes. But when she turned this time, she saw nothing but an encroaching fog. It swirled around her, thick and almost opaque. "Who's there?"

From the shadows two forms emerged. The figures of man and a woman, but she couldn't make out their features.

"Turn around and see the future," the woman said in a soft voice.

Tnasha did as instructed and realized that she could no longer see the ocean or the cliffs a dangerous step away; she could only hear the waves crashing against the crags below. Behind her, two sets of footfalls stopped short, mere inches from her. She could hear their breathing.

The woman whispered softly into her ear, "Step into eternity, child." With a firm shove, Tnasha felt herself fall over the edge of the cliff. The wind rushed past her face as the sound of the waves crashing against the cliffs grew louder. Her eyes flew open. With her heart pounding in her chest and her breath raspy and caught in her throat, she looked around. Shanalyn placed a gentle arm beneath her shoulders and brought her into a sitting position. "Relax, Tnasha. It was only a dream."

"No, it wasn't!"

Shanalyn, the youthful priestess who had been left to watch after Tnasha, jumped back and her jaw dropped open. She moved back to Tnasha's side, disbelief covering her face. "You are sitting by yourself! You're speaking!"

Tnasha's mana began moving again. At first, the violet mana twisted slowly, churning like a thousand chaotic tornadoes. But slowly, ever so slowly, the pattern of mana changed and shifted, cleared and began moving evenly, clockwise around her body. She took a deep breath, all at once realizing she needed to relieve her bladder. She forced her legs over the side of the bed.

"Say something else," Shanalyn prodded. Her blond hair was disheveled, and her pale cheeks had a flush to them.

Tnasha looked into Shanalyn's blue, pleading eyes filled half with excitement, half fear. "What do you want me to say? I need to use the chamber pot, quickly."

Shanalyn ignored the request and threw her arms around Tnasha, embracing her in a tight hug. "That's fine!"

Still feeling weak, Tnasha gently pushed Shanalyn back. "I still need to be able to breathe and urinate."

Apologetically, Shanalyn pulled back. "I must tell your family and the physician, and Priestess Caitlan," she said, her voice taking on a lyrical, high-pitched excitement.

"Could you please wait?" Tnasha let out a deep exhale. "I need time to acclimate."

Shanalyn's face fell, causing her smooth pale skin to reveal fine lines around the corners of her mouth. "Why?"

"Too many questions at once." Tnasha tried to stand. "If your reaction is telling of theirs, I will fall back into mana paralysis."

Shanalyn let out a nervous laugh. "Don't say that, ever. Not even in jest. Do you not want to see them?"

She ran a hand through her auburn hair, feeling the weight of it. "You know my family. They must be taken in moderation. The physician will only poke at me, and Priestess Caitlan will ask me spiritual questions I'm unprepared for. Like some horrible type of litmus test to make sure I'm not possessed and in my right mind."

After taking a moment to think about it, Shanalyn agreed with a nod. "I understand."

"I just need awhile to readjust to being able to move." She lifted her arm, feeling the ache in her weak muscles.

"You will still need movement therapy before you're better. You'll also have to limit the use of your mana." Shanalyn's voice had taken on a mothering tone as she retrieved the chamber pot, handing the oblong receptacle for Tnasha and steadying her while she moved to use it.

Tnasha lifted an eyebrow, feeling the muscle twitch. She sighed with relief, and noticed her facial muscles tired easily. "I had no intention of using my mana or getting physical."

"Good. Your body will regenerate itself faster if you don't." Shanalyn took the chamber pot and set it on the table near the door.

"I can't believe how much time I've lost to this." Tnasha rubbed her hands together, pushing the cold from them and urging the blood in.

"Lost? Only a month." A small smile played on Shanalyn's pink lips.

"It felt like years." Her eyes wandered back to the Eagle's Talon and she sat back down on the bed and drew her legs up. It seemed odd to see it sitting there so informally.

Shanalyn followed her gaze and helped her back into the bed, drawing the blankets back over her. "What is that, anyway? Did someone make you a walking stick? It's pretty."

"That's not a walking stick. It's the Eagle's Talon," Tnasha said with a gruff edge to her voice. She was almost offended by Shanalyn's lack of respect for the staff, but then realized the priestess didn't know any better. Her tone softened. "It's actually a stave of great power as it allows one to see into the present and the future."

She didn't bother to tell Shanalyn that it was possible the Eagle's Talon did much more, mostly because she still wasn't sure of the full scope of the staff's power, or how to use it.

"Does it work?" Shanalyn walked over to it and reached out her hand, touching the black stone grasped in the Eagle's talon. Then she picked it up.

Panic welled in Tnasha's chest. "Yes. It turns gray when it is being used. Please hand it here. You shouldn't touch it."

She remembered back to how the staff made her feel when she used it. Her entire body vibrated with its essence, as if she and the staff merged somehow. In Shanalyn's grasp, however, it appeared neutral.

"Where did you find it?" Her eyes were wide with curiosity.

Tnasha took another deep breath, then let it out slowly. It felt good to breathe deeply. She reached out for the staff. "In Arkeereon, with the other two. The Crow's Foot, and the Raven's Claw."

Shanalyn pursed her lips, giving her a questioning look. Then she handed staff over.

"No more questions. I don't have the energy to answer." She let out an unbidden yawn and drew the staff to her chest.

"As you wish. Do you want me to go?"

Tnasha had mixed feelings about this. She wanted the company, but at the same time, she wanted time to think, feel, move. "Maybe you could go for a little while. But I want you to come back."

Priestess Shanalyn smiled. "All right. I will come back in several hours."

Tnasha watched her leave, taking the chamber pot with her. After the door closed and the room fell silent, Tnasha held the staff next to her as if to protect it. Her thoughts went back to the dream. "Step into eternity?" she asked herself in barely a whisper. Her brown eyes peered into the stone atop the Eagle's Talon, deep in thought. If she could just use it to see what was coming next... but she stopped herself. She knew the power the staff held and knew that if she started relying on it for every little thing, she would become dependent on it. Addicted. Kalath had once warned her never to use divination for every little decision, or, without one's tools, one would become paralyzed with indecision. She assumed the same would apply to the staff. So she relaxed back into the pillows and frowned at the magical artifact, wondering what would happen now. With all she knew and everything she'd been through, there was nowhere to go except forward into the promise of a dangerous future.

CHAPTER 2

The hierarchs who sat around the large, circular, dark wood table appeared tired and wary. Natyis' gaze went around the table, pausing on each of them briefly. All of them his closest confidants and friends. They'd been arguing for hours

Sven, tall and thin, narrowed his black eyes. He had been most quiet of all, but he was also the one who always deeply considered everything Natyis said. "You think *she* is *Delepitoré*, your ancestor, re-born."

Sven knew him so well. While Natyis did think the Danarian sorceress, Tnasha, bore the mana of the goddess Delepitoré and of someone he once knew who had died long ago, he knew better. Despite the Arkeeronish custom of naming children after the gods their mana most represented, none of the mage-born were gods themselves. Natyis merely shook his head at Sven.

The room fell silent. Luithian's gray eyes went wide and the water sorcerer straightened in his chair. "This has nothing to do with Aithian at all."

Luithian was also right. How could Natyis explain to them something he couldn't see clearly but could feel? The hierarchy was used to Natyis' visions being clear and concise. Where the Danarian sorceress was concerned, however, Natyis was blind. Her mana blocked him from seeing her future and the events that surrounded her. Even though he could not see things clearly, he knew that they needed her. Somehow, she could save them. He could feel it. The mana compatibility and mutual attraction between Aithian and Tnasha had to play into that. It made sense. Natyis tilted his dark head of gray streaked hair forward. "I assure you, I am thinking of her and Aithian alike. And a possible alliance with the Danarian families. We need her."

"You realize that if even if she does have the mana of Delepitore, by flesh and blood she is not your ancestor." Sven seemed stuck on that point.

Natyis' white eyes clouded over, looking almost gray. He frowned. "Yes."

The door to the chamber opened and Unsere, aptly named for her deep green mana that matched the attributes of the goddess *Unsere*, entered without announcement. "Would you prefer your mid-day meal in here, or in the dining hall?"

"We would have preferred you knocked." Natyis scowled at his wife without really meaning to do so.

"I *have* been knocking. Evidently you couldn't hear it." With hands on her hips she gave him a dark look.

"I apologize, Lady Unsere. I put wards on the room to keep our conversation private," Eury said. An abashed grin covered his face.

"Yes. Well, we will eat in here." Natyis wasn't in the mood to argue with her.

"Fine. I'll bring it in shortly." She turned toward the door.

"No."

She turned back to him like a cobra that threatened to strike.

Natyis softened his tone. "Please send Aithian to bring it in. We'd like to speak with him."

Unsere relented and visibly relaxed. "I don't think he is feeling well today. I haven't seen him up and about."

"Regardless, please ask him to join us. It's rather important." Then, in an effort to save himself the cold shoulder later, Natyis added quickly, "Thank you."

"Very well." She closed the door behind her.

Natyis looked over his hierarchy of sorcerers, meeting each set of eyes with a knowing look. Then he said, "We all know it's the right thing to do."

"Do we?" Luithian asked.

"You have to trust me. Have I ever led any of you astray?" Natyis felt a pang of guilt in his gut. He didn't like it either, but he had to talk to Tnasha, to figure out why he couldn't see anything around her. To find out how she was going to help them.

"I vote for sending a message to the sorceress and her family and inviting them here," Sven said, knowing full well that wasn't an option.

"I told you - the situation is dire. We don't have time for that," Natyis countered, exasperated. He closed his eyes. "Eury, please take down the wards."

"I already did," the funerary priest said.

Just then, a stiff knock sounded from the other side of the door.

"Enter." Natyis sat back, overlooking the hierarchs whose attention stood focused on the door. For the past half-hour they'd gone over the entire plan and had *mostly* agreed with Natyis' thoughts on the matter. In order to save themselves, they'd have to bring Tnasha here through magical means, and then convince her that she wanted to stay. Aithian, and the attraction between them, was key to the plan.

Aithian entered, carrying a platter filled with meat, cheese, fruit, vegetables and a loaf of bread. He set the platter on the table then turned and closed the door. "You wanted to see me?"

"Sit down, Aithian." Natyis leaned forward and looked into the young man's eyes. Aithian, Luithian's son, was also a water sorcerer. At scarcely twenty-four, the young man's azure eyes were sullen. The hierarchs had raised their children with plenty of pragmatism and too little hope for the future.

Wordlessly, Aithian did as instructed, and looked at each of them with dark curiosity.

Natyis gave Aithian a forced smile. "We have decided to bring the Danarian sorceress, Tnasha, here."

Aithian furrowed his brow but said nothing.

"We're hoping to match you with her. If it works out, she will be yours." There was a note of finality to Natyis' voice.

"Wait - you mean to kidnap her and bring her here against her will?" His expression sat somewhere between amusement and horror at the idea.

"She will learn to adapt," Natyis said, his voice unsure. His stomach twisted again.

Aithian laughed. "I don't think you understand *her will.* You can't just force someone…"

Natyis cut him off. "Her will does not matter at this point. If necessary, we will neutralize her mana until she comes around to our way of thinking."

Grunts of disapproval sounded from around the table.

"Her will matters to me. She will never agree to bond with me like this." Folding his arms across his chest, he glowered and gave Natyis a defiant look.

"Your father," Natyis nodded toward Luithian who was shaking his head, "…much like you, is against the idea despite the fact that he was the one to initially suggest it. Unfortunately, most of us agree that it must be done. My sight says she is the key to our immediate survival, which means it's the only way to secure the bloodline. Bring in new blood."

Eury straightened in his chair and cleared his throat. "I do not recall a decision actually being made. We merely discussed the plan and any potential consequences if things didn't quite go our way."

Natyis stood and slammed his fist on the table, causing everyone in the room to jump, startled. "I have led our families through difficult times and never have I been wrong! *I am not wrong this time.*"

Aithian leaned forward and buried his head in his hands. "You have kept us from the outside world. It would be just as easy to make friends with the Danarians. Go for a visit, and perhaps *ask* if she was interested in coming out here."

"Where we would be considered outsiders, possibly invaders?" Natyis scoffed. "Besides, we don't have time. We need her here immediately."

"Yet you cannot tell us why," Luithian said, clearly frustrated.

"Waiting and going about this in a more civilized way would be better than abducting her. If we do this, we're no better than the

Kersians," Aithian said, then added with a mournful look, "And there would be no way she would ever trust me."

"We can make her family believe she has come to us of her own free will. In the end she will stay by choice." Natyis was sure this is what had to happen. He felt it would work even though he couldn't see the specifics. Despite the accuracy of his visions in the past, his own people still balked. Maybe they sensed his frustration in not being able to see it all clearly.

Aithian furrowed his dark brow and scowled.

"Speak your mind, son." Natyis let out a heavy sigh. "It still amazes me that even though I've never led any of you astray, that my sight is still so mistrusted."

The young man, Aithian, shook his head. "When your visions go against what feels right, it's only natural for us to resist them. They're counter-intuitive. We also know you're not one to change your mind, and that ultimately it is your decision as elder. Our agreement isn't necessary."

Luithian nodded in agreement and leaned forward. "Not to mention the last time we disagreed, even though things turned out as you said they would, there was a brief time where it didn't look like they would."

"That's because there will always be struggle along the way. We need to have faith in our young ones that they are able to be strong and conquer their fears. We need to trust that they will prevail." Then Natyis smiled. Not because he was happy with how the conversation was turning out, but because he knew he was right. He trusted the sons of Arkeereon far more than their own fathers did.

Aithian let out a resigned sigh. "Fine. But remember that I didn't agree."

"Yet you want her." Natyis knew that to be true. He had seen the way Aithian and Tnasha looked at one another. There was a *mana-spark* there, the term the elders used for a good match.

"Not against her will." Aithian looked at the men around the table as if waiting for one of them to say something against Natyis. But no one did.

"Her will shall become ours," Natyis assured everyone. Then he turned to Aithian. "We haven't even considered the possibility that

perhaps she wants to be here with you. This would give her an excuse."
He kept smiling, feeling the grin growing more solid on his face.

Aithian set his jaw and stood, and then began passing around
the plates of food. "We should start eating before Lady Unsere comes
back to check on us."

Lord Eury chuckled, and that seemed to ease the tension in the
room. "We certainly don't want to upset *her*." He paused long enough
to meet Natyis' gaze. Then he added, "Or *any* woman in this holding
for that matter. They are, after all, self-regenerative whereas we are
not."

Lord Sven nodded in agreement. "Without females we would
all suffer imbalance and there would be no family lines to speak of."

"So, what is it you are trying to say?" Natyis took a bite of
cheese.

Luithian was the first to respond. "Perhaps this should be
discussed with everyone before we proceed. *Including* the women."

"The women would have my head." Natyis wasn't smiling
anymore. He knew none of the women would agree, especially his wife,
who, if he told her what they planned to do, would give him a tongue
lashing. Of course, she would find out anyway. Sometimes the only
way to deal with situations like this was to rip off the bandage and
expose the wound so it could heal. Natyis glanced up. The looks on
their faces asked just how long he thought he could keep something
like this from their wives and daughters. "Fine, I'll tell the women."

Sven shook his head. Natyis knew then that he was
outnumbered not only among his hierarchy, but among everyone else
who lived in Arkeereon's great holding as well.

CHAPTER 3

After killing his brother, Gavgal, and taking over Zul, the Kersian sorcerer Seth had a throne made for himself. It stood on the far wall of the great hall against a backdrop of deep red and gold tapestries made of fine silk. The throne itself was hand-carved of oak, and it was gilded and inlaid with the symbol of the Unnamed God on its back. The sovereign chair sat upon a raised platform, so he could look down at his subjects like a god might. The Unnamed God was a thing Seth cared little about, but his subjects' belief in it did an adequate job of keeping them subservient. Religion had proved itself a scepter of power that Seth wielded like a hammer.

Now, two priests scurried behind him as he approached the new seat of power, their eyes downcast and obedient. Stepping onto the platform, Seth sat down upon the deep crimson cushioned chair, enjoying the view it gave him. Wiping imaginary dust from his black tunic, he sat erect and straightened the lacing straps down the front. Then he ran his hands over his close-cut blond hair. He'd taken care to look the part of emperor and had made his maid polish his black leather boots twice, and iron his leggings. Sure that his appearance was in proper order, he appraised his subjects with a critical eye.

Guards clad in black with red jerkins stood ready to Seth's left and his right.

"Summon my brother, Alax," he snapped at one of the men closest to him.

The faithful Kersian soldier hurried from the room to do Seth's bidding. It wasn't like Seth had to specify which brother to summon anymore. Alax was the only one left.

"Your Eminence…" one of the priests started. The priests wore long, bland black robes with no markings, but both wore gold colored amulets with the Unnamed God's symbol on them.

Seth flicked a hand at them. "Silence."

"But this is important, Sire." The man lowered his bald head, likely fearing retribution.

Truly, Seth was far more volatile than Gavgal had been, but then Gavgal was weak. Seth was strong. Now bored, Seth put on a smile laden with superiority. "Entertain me."

"Our intelligence has gathered that your brother, Morvack, has pledged his allegiance to the Imperial Hierarchy of the Arkeeronish. They offered him a wife in exchange."

Seth let out a half laugh, half growl. "Why am I not surprised? I assumed he had not survived. I suppose I underestimated him, and yet Morvack was always such a simpleton. Simple minded and easily bribed. With a woman. Ha. I could have given him that."

"Our agents fear that this may signal the beginnings of our defeat." The priest gave Seth a defiant look, then quickly realized his place, lowered his eyes, and took a step back.

Seth stood. "Defeat?" He stepped down from his platform and leaned in toward the priest only inches from him. "Hear this and spread it well. The Kersian Empire does not need fools like Gavgal and Morvack. With them, we merely stood our ground. With my leadership and Alax's ability to persuade the people, we will take all of The West Ocean Mainlands under our wing, and I shall rule as Emperor."

The second priest, a younger man with a head full of brown hair, cleared his throat. "With all due respect, your eminence, The Unnamed is the only Emperor. You can merely be but his vessel, the one through which he speaks."

Seth turned on his heel to face the insolent man before him. "You mistake me for someone who believes in your imaginary deity. I am deity now, and I have a name. Guards."

Soldiers sworn to Seth alone came forward from their stations on either side of the platform. "Arrest this infidel and have him put to death. I do not have time for insolence nor invisible Gods." Then he turned to the older priest. "Are you amiable to my cause? Or would you challenge me, too?"

"No, sire." The priest cowered, his mouth a grim line. The fire that had been in his eyes only minutes before vanished completely.

"Good."

The young man tried to fight, but the soldiers were stronger. As the soldiers dragged the young priest away, Seth turned to his remaining audience. The older priest, one of his Generals, and a serving maid stood at attention, their faces blank. Seth cleared his throat. He wanted to make sure they all understood him clearly. "Learn from his example. Anyone who opposes me will die."

A heinous grin slid over Seth's face. His vast armies sided with him thanks to Alax's persuasion, outnumbering the population of Zul. He had no problems eliminating anyone who stood in his way.

Alax, with his mop of brown hair uncombed and his tunic rumpled, entered the room just as the apprehended priest was escorted out. He lifted a curious brow. "Treason?"

Seth nodded, looking Alax up and down. "How perceptive of you."

"I suspected as much," Alax said, not acknowledging anyone else in the room, nor the disapproving look of his brother.

"It seems our brother Morvack is alive and living well with a wife in Arkeereon." Seth studied Alax's reaction.

"Oh?"

"Yes."

Alax let out an annoyed sigh. "He was always weak that way."

"That's what I said. Do you desire a wife, brother?" He had never imagined Alax with a wife or a family.

"We must continue our family lines, so I suppose it would be necessary. Eventually." Alax appeared bored.

Seth smiled. That was exactly the reaction he expected from Alax. "I suppose you're right. Which is why I have taken the liberty of sending soldiers to the Angoran territories. They should arrive within the week with several females. If one doesn't suit my purposes, you may have her. I have considered the possibility that I would need a son to take my place someday. Though I wish now that I had taken the sorceress when I had a chance."

Alax snorted in a most undignified way. "She would have been too defiant for breeding stock."

"Perhaps. Even so, now we shall have the females we need to start anew. If Morvack survived, is it possible she may have survived as well?" Seth didn't wait for an answer. His smile spread wider growing smug at the thought. "Well, it's not matter. We shall deal with that issue when we finally take Danaria. If she did survive, I will force her into submission and make her one of my consorts. No doubt our victory might curb some of that aggression she harbors."

"As was Gavgal's plan," Alax said with a raised brow.

Seth narrowed his eyes. Did Alax think Seth was anything like Gavgal? He fumed at the thought. "Gavgal's desire to continue our family lines took precedence over his lust for power, brother. *That* is what led to his ruin." Seth licked his dry, cracked lips. "He could not have conceived an heir regardless. He was impotent. Why do you think he killed our mother, sisters, and the other sorceresses born as Kersians?"

Alax continued to show little emotion. "I suspected as much."

Seth paused, deciding it not prudent to speak of family secrets so openly amongst the servants. He snapped his fingers and the serving girl was instantly at his side. "Girl, get my brother and I, and the General, some wine. Priest - leave us," Seth ordered with another dismissive flick of his hand.

The girl hurried to the table and poured three glasses of wine as the remaining priest all but ran from the room with his head down. She returned quickly and gave one glass to Alax, and one to the General who had been quiet the entire time. The girl handed Seth his glass last. She was fortunate he had more important things to worry about, otherwise he would have flogged her for such an oversight. "With as much as you suspect, Alax, you should share your suspicions with me more often."

"I would hate to be presumptuous."

"We still have Exavia. As I see it, we should take Cabalia and Arkeereon first, then maybe Sherok and Carinth. Though three of those are human territories and worthless beyond their natural resources. Regardless the method of attack, I am confident we can overthrow Danaria. They will come to see things my way."

"If I may *suspect* once more?"

"By all means, brother."

"We do not have enough sorcery between the mere two of us to wage war upon hundreds, possibly thousands of sorcerers. It would be suicide. Much like sending troops to the Angoran territories likely is. How many do you think will return from that mission? As much as I didn't care for Gavgal, I believe his plan in building an army of sorcerers was a more logical one."

Seth fought back the urge to berate his younger brother. How dare he question his plan to harvest Angoran sorcerer females? It would work, wouldn't it? Inside his head, a cloud of self-doubt began to loom. He brushed it aside and said, "It could take years to sway sorcerers and train them to my way of thinking. My plan is more efficient. We shall build our own mana weapon, something more powerful than the Raven's Claw. More powerful than anything Gavgal could conceive." This was something Seth had been thinking about for some time.

"Do we have the means by which to do such a thing?"

"Of course, we do. Our private library is full of our ancestral grimoires, books Gavgal banned for the sake of continuing his false religion. Religion can only adequately control the masses for so long. To truly control the people, they need to see real power and sheer force. Which is why anyone who opposes us shall die." Seth lifted the wine glass to his lips and sucked down the sweet dry liquid. Then he licked his lips again. "Perhaps we could even test your powers of persuasion on a larger scale."

Alax did not appear to be convinced. Seth knew Alax's powers didn't work on those with the mage-blood, but he knew it worked on smaller groups of humans. He'd seen it.

Alax looked around the great hall and finally asked, "So if we can create this weapon, how will we test it?"

"We could go to Corinth, but again, *humans*. Perhaps I should just eliminate Corinth from the plan entirely. Perhaps we need to start in Arkeereon."

"Why Arkeereon?"

"Around eighty sorcerers live behind those walls. We can distract the men, take the women, then use the weapon to destroy the city and the males. Or would you have us try to get the males to agree to fight for our cause and swear their allegiance to me?"

Amusement passed quickly over Alax's face, then vanished. "Perhaps we should take the younger males prisoner even if they do not agree to your terms. We cannot have an inbred family line." Alax furrowed his brow. "Young males are impressionable enough that we could restructure their way of thinking."

Seth's stony stare bore into Alax. "Are you serious, or are you trying to save lives?" When Alax didn't respond to the question, Seth relented. He needed his brother's support. "As I said, that could take years, but have it your way, brother. I'm willing to compromise. We have holding cells and I've seen ways of neutralizing mana presented in the grimoires."

"If it didn't work, we could kill them," Alax said, as if he could read Seth's mind.

Though Seth's features remained cool, relief wash over him. The last thing he needed was Alax going soft on him. "Very well. Perhaps later this evening you could join me in the library. After you've cleaned yourself up, of course. We should start with the weapon immediately."

Alax lifted a wary brow, completely ignoring Seth's comment about his appearance. "Is there an alternate plan? Just in case something goes wrong, and we are forced into doing something different?"

"You worry too much. It doesn't become you." With that, Seth took a long drink of the wine, feeling it calm his nerves.

"I would much rather be prepared. It's not that I doubt your plan, but situations change," Alax said.

"Indeed, they do," Seth said, taking another long drink.

Alax looked over at the General, who had not said anything during the entire conversation. "And the General?"

"I have not forgotten you," Seth said, nodding at the General. "If anyone opposes my leadership, have them imprisoned. They will be made to stand before me for judgment." Seth stood and straightened his belt.

The General nodded. "Yes, Emperor."

Seth grinned. "I like the sound of that." He turned to the serving maid standing off to the side with folded hands and bowed head. "You, girl. See to it that the evening meal is started on, then come to my chambers and draw my bath."

Obediently, she left. Seth took the last gulp of wine, draining the cup as the others hastily finished theirs and departed his throne room. He drew in a cleansing breath and closed his eyes. There, in his mind's eye, he watched his plan come together. Although still chaotic and not fully realized, it would come to fruition. He knew it.

CHAPTER 4

"Tnasha seems healthy enough. I only wish I knew *how* her mana started moving again." The physician, a thin, short man, sat back on his heels, looking up at Lord Termark who stood tall above him.

"I don't care how it started. I am merely happy my daughter is alive and well." Termark's concern shown itself in the weathered creases of his face. In the dim afternoon light that streamed through the window, his dark ash brown, shoulder-length hair looked almost black.

The physician, who had been kneeling at her bedside, lifted himself to his feet. "I will check in on her again in a few days. If there are any problems before then, send a messenger for me."

Tnasha rolled her eyes. After he was gone, she turned to her father with a wry smile. "What is the purpose of calling a physician if he doesn't have the first idea how to treat mana disorders?"

Termark shrugged. He pulled the small wooden chair that sat next to the window nearer her bed and sat down, causing the chair to creak under the weight of his sturdy, muscular frame. He set his strong jaw and looked at his daughter with intense brown eyes. "Peace of mind," he finally said. "It makes your mother and I feel better knowing he's seen you."

"You mean the physician made *you* feel better. The *priestesses* made mother feel better."

He chuckled. "That is probably a better way to put it."

21

"You heard that Kalath is dead?" In a moment of melancholy, a tear escaped the corner of her eye, but she quickly wiped it away and put on a brave face.

Termark's tone turned somber. "I know."

"He was like a grandfather to me." She stated it plainly rather than give into the deep swell of sorrow and loss she felt each time she thought of Kalath. She couldn't cry. If she did, she would succumb to the numbness that followed, and there was no time for that. She needed to be strong now.

"Yes."

"I was unable to kill Seth. He's too strong." She involuntarily frowned at her own failure.

A dark look overcame Termark at the mention of Seth. "The Sorcerer Seth is… insane. The insanity increases his mana strength."

"How?"

"People like him find pleasure in death, war, and feeling powerful. Whereas in others, these things invoke fear and feelings of powerlessness." Her father shrugged.

A swell of anger rushed through her. "I'd like to strip him down, tie him to a tree, and use him for target practice."

Termark laughed, smoothing the tension. "I know many people who would pay a week's wages for that opportunity. Morvack's armies were passive. But Seth's armies-they are the ones you have to watch for. They're aggressive and bold. We've heard from our inside informant that he sent two legions into the Angoran territories."

"Well, Morvack's armies are no more, at least," she said with optimism, as if pointing this out somehow made Seth's armies appear less threatening. It didn't.

"Yes, I heard Morvack was killed." Termark flexed his hand as if he were choking the life from someone, then drew his fingers into a fist.

"No, he's not dead. Morvack converted. Or switched allegiances. I suppose both are correct. He's in Arkeereon now. With the Imperial Hierarchy. He's taking one of their daughters as his wife."

Termark's mouth dropped open in disbelief. After a moment of uncomfortable silence, he said, "Well - I never imagined it possible."

"Neither did I. I think when he realized his insane brother wanted to kill him, he decided he was on the wrong side." She let out a heavy sigh. "But you know what's really strange?"

"Hmm?"

"He wasn't a bad person to begin with. All he ever wanted was a family. That's not evil or wrong." She thought back to Morvack and how docile he seemed in the presence of the Hierarchy. It seemed all he wanted to do was melt away into obscurity. She didn't blame him. If she could have done the same, she would have.

"You would be amazed at what motivates a person to do something that others perceive as evil. If Gavgal held the promise of a family over Morvack's head, and Morvack saw no other way, that would be enough to keep his allegiance," her father said with a deeply exhaled sigh.

Her eyes wandered to the Eagle's Talon. "It's one of their ancestral artifacts. Why don't we have contact with the families in Arkeereon? I mean, we talk to the Angorans all the time, even though they prefer living in the mountains like nomads."

"The Angorans feel safer there." He nodded. "From what I've heard about the families in Arkeereon, a very old dispute has kept all of us apart. So old, in fact, that I doubt anyone remembers what it was about. But you know, their families are not native to Arkeereon. They're Sherokean."

This information wasn't new to her or anyone else. The dark hair and eyes that were predominant among them identified them as such. There were a few anomalies among them. "I should take the staff back to them." She stretched her arms and yawned.

"Don't worry about the staff. You need to get well first. The maids will be drawing your bath soon, and then you can have a meal. Get more rest." He stood.

"All right." She watched him leave, then once he had left the room and closed the door behind him, she sat up and brought her legs over the side of the bed. She stood. Her legs wobbled from lack of use, feeling weak and unstable, but the priestesses had been sure to move them while she had been paralyzed, to keep the muscles from becoming atrophied. Slowly, she made her way to the staff, and picked it up. She carried it back to the bed and sat down, holding it. Images of Aithian flooded her memory. He was strong and quiet. A shiver of excitement ran through her. For the first time in her life, she wondered what a man was thinking of her instead of whether or not she could best him in combat. "I wonder what he thinks of me?" she whispered to herself. She decided then that the minute she felt up to it, she would take the staff back to Arkeereon if for no other reason than to see Aithian again.

The maids entered then. The swishing of their skirts pulled her from her thoughts. She set the staff beside her on the bed, then stood, allowing them to help her to the bathing room.

After bathing and eating, Tnasha lay on top of the thick quilts covering her bed and stared up at the ceiling, feeling her eyes grow heavy. Shanalyn sat beside her.

"You should sleep."

Tnasha's voice came out barely a whisper. "Step into eternity. What do you think that means?"

Shanalyn shrugged her shoulders. "How should I know?"

Tnasha yawned again. "You're the priestess. You should be able to interpret something like that."

"We are all eternal and part of all that is." There was a sense of finality to her answer.

"So, I should step into myself?"

"To know thyself is to know the nature of everything around you."

In Tnasha's experience, the clergy often said things like this. Besides, Shanalyn's statement was something she'd heard before. "From your own perspective, which is unique from anyone else's? If that's the case, there is no truth."

"Some truths are subjective and vary based on the individual." Shanalyn's voice was tinged with amusement now.

Tnasha shook her head. The dream still made little sense, and Shanalyn was not helping. "Maybe I should step into sleep."

"That's what I just said."

"No, you said... never mind. Will you come tomorrow?" Tnasha asked through a yawn.

"Of course. Do you think I would actually abandon you to Priestess Caitlan and a long line of anonymous visitors?"

"I would hope not." Tnasha smiled and yawned again.

Shanalyn laughed, stood, and left the room, leaving Tnasha to fall into a deep sleep. As she fell further and further into the blackness, her dreams took her to Arkeereon.

She knocked on the rough, decrepit wooden doors of their holding, carrying the staff in one hand. The doors appeared to tower high above her, disappearing into the looming, suffocating darkness all around her. "I have your staff. I have brought it back to return it!" she screamed at the doors.

Fog hung low to the ground, obscuring the moat and the bridge she stood on. A deafening, grave silence overwhelmed her.

"Step into eternity," a woman's voice said. "The Eagle's Talon, look at it. The stone becomes gray… Eagle's Talon, Gray."

Her eyes searched the fog for some sign of the owner of the voice, but she found no one. She turned around to find herself facing Aithian, drawn to his fierce blue eyes. He took her in his arms, pressed his lips to hers, and held her close to his body. Then everything faded black and she was nothing more than a pinpoint of light in a vast space of nothing.

CHAPTER 5

Unsere, wearing a pale blue dress that flattered her petite frame, tapped one small leather clad foot impatiently on the marble floor. She absently shoved a long strand of black and gray hair behind her ear. Lord Natyis, her husband of over forty years, sat before her in a simple cross frame chair, leaning his chin on his hands, his pale eyes boring into the maroon rug at his feet. Despite his age, his frame was still sturdy and his muscles firm, and his current idea - still disturbingly rash.

Unsere could not hold her tongue any longer. "I find it dismaying. How would you like it if Danaria took me?" she asked.

"That's different." His white eyes did not avert from the rug.

Her eyes darkened, and her look turned steely. "How is it different? You're plotting to take a woman from her home and family in order to use her as breeding stock!"

"So, you disagree?"

She stiffened, her brown eyes growing wide. "You have the audacity to ask me if I disagree? By the *Elders of The Watch,* I swear, Natyis! There are more diplomatic ways. I would have expected better from you. Not this."

He finally looked up, lifting an eyebrow. "You expect me to try to arrange a formal marriage through letters and couriers?"

"As the civilized world does. Yes." Unsere let out an irritated sigh.

"And what if the answer is no? We are not dealing with a highly cultured society, Unsere. These people have a society built on their military. They are barbaric and, I would think, more likely to arrange marriages within local family castes rather than with foreign ones."

"But what if they agreed?" She crossed her arms over her chest.

"The chances are slim."

"You will start a war. Then our family lines will die because it seems to me we would be grossly outnumbered." Exasperated, she threw up her hands and began pacing.

Natyis scowled and turned his attention back to the rug. "This is a difficult situation, Unsere. One you clearly don't understand."

"Of course, I don't. After all, I am but a mere woman." She set her jaw and scowled back at him. "Do what you will, but I warn you now, Natyis. If the Danarians wage war upon us, myself and the other women will surrender unconditionally. There is no need for us to willingly march to the slaughter. Even alleged barbarians value alliances."

He shook his head. "How would you know?"

"They have not tried to overthrow Carinth, Cabalia, Sherok, or Arkeereon, have they? They are not a country that propagates war. As I see it, their military is strong because it has to be. For protection. They're defensive, not offensive. Consider it."

Letting out a resigned sigh, his voice softened. "It *has* been considered."

"I'm going to bed." She turned to leave.

"Wait," he said, his voice lowering. "I was enjoying our debate."

"Debating with you is much like…" She stopped herself and took a moment to regain her composure. "Never mind."

The nerve of that man, she thought. How could she love a man who made her so angry? But then she knew the answer to that. Natyis had swept her off her feet and read her poetry, and he'd always been gentle and kind. That's when she realized, with some sadness, that he wouldn't have devised such a plan unless their circumstances were dire. This thought alone sent a shiver of fear up her spine.

***

After his wife left, Natyis leaned back in his chair and pressed the fleshy part of his palms into his eyes, allowing colorful fractals to fill the darkness beneath his lids. Unsere was right. Diplomacy could have worked, but there wasn't enough time for that. A queasy feeling entered his stomach. He'd attempted to divine the situation again, but the results were still the same. He could not see anything around the sorceress clearly. He only knew that he could *feel* two outcomes. Bringing the sorceress here brought about a safer, warmer feeling, leading him to believe that this was the most favorable solution. He had not told the other hierarchs because he could not lie to them. In turn they would not understand why he could not see clearly. This was the easiest way. There was no room for failure. They needed Tnasha more than her own people needed her.

He stood. Luithian and Eury, though they also disagreed, would be meeting him in the temple where they would perform the ritual. Once they had her, the girl would agree to write a letter stating her intention to marry Aithian. Her family would have to agree then. Especially if a marriage rite had already sanctified the union.

"No room for failure," he said to himself.

With that, he rose from his chair and started toward the temple. The others would be there already.

Inside the temple, the ceilings rose high above them. High, cathedral windows towered on either side, allowing moonlight to cast its eerie light along the marble floors inlaid with sigils of universal god-forms. Eury and Luithian stood in waiting, patient and quiet. Without a word, Natyis approached them.

"How will we do this?" Luithian asked in barely a whisper. He appeared solemn and unsure.

Natyis gave him an encouraging smile. "This is not a funeral, Luithian. Cheer up."

Eury smirked. "We're abducting a woman, which could lead to our own funerals."

"I see everyone is against me." He averted his eyes to the ground, trying to decide where he should stand.

"Not you." Eury assured him. "The decision to do this."

"If we try political means, and they respond unfavorably, and then we took her, they would know it was us. At least this way we have a chance. We can continue our family lines. Perhaps force an alliance that will bring us more females." Natyis knew his explanation was poor at best.

"It is no longer about the mana?"

With a sideway glance Natyis said, "Of course it is, but you need to see the larger picture. It has always been about our survival."

Eury gave up and turned to Luithian, who stood shivering. "It's freezing in here."

Obliging, Natyis threw a mana blate into the hearth, setting aflame the logs inside. "We should do this now."

Luithian's voice emerged almost a whisper. "There's no turning back once we start."

Natyis shook his head. "No."

They stood an equal distance from one another, forming a triangle. Natyis lifted his arms, "I call to you, powers of earth, be present in your element. Come forth in protection and aid us."

Eury cleared his throat, following suit. "I call to you, powers of air, be present in your element. Come forth in protection and aid us."

"I call to you, powers of fire, be present in your element. Come forth in protection and aid us." Luithian quickly bowed his head and lowered his arms.

Natyis then called on water, Eury life, and Luithian death. Lastly, the forces of healing, destruction, and the whole were called. Now, all nine divinities, in nine colors of independent mana, swirled about them, bouncing off each of their bodies and forming a triangular pattern of light between them. A chaotic energy permeated the air, all at once culminating into crisp, clean lines of rainbow color creating the final and well-defined triangle of light necessary to draw the sorceress through the portal.

Luithian fell to his knees, gasped for air, then heaved clear syrupy liquid onto the polished black marble floor. This did not diminish the mana they'd called upon. Though he shook, Luithian still sat in the same spot, grounding the energy. The lines remained solid and steady.

Natyis' voice echoed through the temple, low and foreboding. "By the Eagle's Talon, carved by the hands of our ancestors, we call you Tnasha fen'Schoitt. Come to us willingly. Focus on her."

The others obeyed his order, imagining the young woman with auburn hair, deep brown eyes, and violet mana. It was not long before her image, a compilation of will and visualization, lay huddled on the cold floor within the triangle. Her form seemed ethereal, translucent.

"Come to us, through the folds of space and time, be present by the names of the elements of our creation!"

The translucent image, beckoned by Natyis, changed then, becoming more opaque and solid until finally, a flash of light burst forth from the center of the triangle, throwing all three men backward onto the ground. The room darkened. There, on the floor between them, the unconscious body of Tnasha lay silent and peaceful. In her hand, she clutched the Eagle's Talon whose once black stone now glowed a soft shade of gray.

Natyis lifted himself from the floor, a look of shock adorning his face. Even with his foresight, part of him never expected it to work. This was the first time he'd ever attempted such a feat of magick. He quickly shook it off. "Come, let us take her to a room. We can impair her mana there."

Eury helped Luithian to his feet. Luithian's face went white when the full implications of the magick they'd just performed dawned on him. "What have we done?"

Natyis answered without a pause. "What we set out to do."

Picking her up, Natyis noticed how light she was. Eury and Luithian followed him to a small chamber in a quiet corridor toward the back of the holding. There, he lay Tnasha's frail, sleeping form on the bed, and drew a blanket over her. He put his hand on her head and closed his eyes. A line of white mana began to circle hers causing her violet mana to shine brilliantly and turn solid. "That should hold her."

Natyis leaned down to her and whispered into her ear, "You chose to come here. For you love Aithian, and you refuse to let anyone tell you otherwise."

Eury, who'd been holding his breath, let his breath out at once. "Do you think it will work?"

Natyis paused before answering. "I guess we will have to wait and see." The three Arkeeronish Sorcerers slipped from the room, locking the door behind them, leaving Tnasha to her dreams, wherein she was still nothing more than a pinpoint of light in a vast void of darkness.

CHAPTER 6

According to Gavgal, the books of their ancestors held dangerous information. They were never to be opened. Watching Seth sift through those books now as if they were common cookbooks unsettled Alax. He bit his tongue to hold back his protests. Gavgal was dead. Zul now obeyed Seth's laws. According to those laws, Seth could do whatever he wished. The books lay open, spread over the table in front of his brother, their dry, yellowing pages caressed by shadows cast from the candlelight and the soft orange glow from the flames of the hearth.

Seth finally looked up from the tomes. "Sit, Alax. I have learned some interesting things about our ancestors. These journals tell me things Gavgal forgot to include in his little speeches."

"Such as?" A genuine look of curiosity crossed Alax's face. He was careful to not provoke his brother's ire and sat as instructed.

"I have told you before that Gavgal was a liar. Our ancestors did not worship an Unnamed God. I find it disconcerting to discover that we were raised with a fabricated religion, don't you?"

Alax found his vocal cords paralyzed. He wasn't sure what Seth wanted him to say.

Luckily Seth took his silence as affirmation. "That is the same reaction I had when I first discovered this. I was speechless."

"Then who or what did we worship?" He was sure he probably already knew the answer, but he had to hear it.

"The very nature of our creation. We were just like those we label heathens." Seth tipped his head, watching Alax for a response.

Alax offered none, not at first. Instead, his mind raced with those things he had done out of belief and loyalty. Lies. His whole life was a lie. At least Seth was willing to speak the truth. Perhaps Seth was not a beast after all, not completely. His face contorted from shock, to confusion, and finally to anger.

Seth turned one of the open books and set it in front of his brother. "Read here, this passage."

Alax's eyes followed Seth's finger. He read it aloud in a dull, flat voice, "For we are as one with all that is as it is with us. Never ending, and eternal. Neither created or destroyed. All that is, simply is. Hence, we hold in high regard those elements of life, as they are ever present around us, and within us. By worshipping them, we worship ourselves as divine creatures of the whole. These things are earth, air, fire, water, life, death, creation, destruction, and the whole. The nine divinities…"

"It seems so strange we were just like all of them once. Reading this has given me new perspective on how to convert the young sorcerers." Seth leaned back on the table. "We are all brethren. Perhaps there is room for us to share our newfound knowledge with some of them." He motioned his hand over the books. "Perhaps if they knew we were more like them, then they would be kinder to our presence and not fight against me as their emperor. It would be easier to convert their young and turn them into our army."

Alax gathered himself and mustered some fake concern. The reality was he could not have cared less. "Are you abandoning the weapon? The plan?"

"Of course not. We need assurance just in case." Seth narrowed his eyes. "I know your powers of persuasion don't work on sorcerers, but perhaps you could try anyway. For all we know, this gift of yours just doesn't work on me."

"What about our people? The ones whose allegiance to us is contingent on an Unnamed God?" Alax fought the urge to sigh heavily and roll his eyes. Had he been braver, less nihilistic, he would have taken Seth by the collar, shook him, and asked his brother if he had any sense.

Seth shook his head, his eyes still narrowed, his lips pulled into a sneer. "You can still use persuasion on them. You simply need to learn to project it more, so you can sway the masses. There may come a time when they discover the truth, and they will want to resurrect Gavgal, so they can kill him again. They will be forever grateful that I... you and I... have brought them the truth. The Unnamed God does not exist, for he only existed in Gavgal's mind."

A shiver of uncertain fear made its way through Alax's body. He had never tried to persuade more than fifty humans at a time, and the idea that he would have to sway thousands didn't sit well with him. Every fiber of Alax's being told him Seth was right, but he knew the people who believed in the Unnamed God were fervent, and they would not give up their deity so easily. It also didn't help that Alax had been raised by Gavgal, who had taught him the same lies. He couldn't help but wonder if the Unnamed God was real, even though his rational mind had always rejected it. Nonetheless, that conditioned fear of the Unnamed, a vengeful God, was still there, arguing with his intellect. "It will take time."

Seth pulled the book back to him, moved around to the other side of the table, and sat in his chair. "It has taken me time to rethink my beliefs as well."

"How long have you known?" Alax was surprised to hear how hollow his own voice sounded. Everything... it was all so pointless.

"Several years now. It was the reason I had to kill him. He was an irrational religious zealot." Seth's dark eyes scanned the page of the book without remorse or feeling.

"Wait. You killed Gavgal?!" It was not so much a question as it was an acknowledgment. This, too, Alax had suspected, but he hadn't been sure until now.

Seth smiled. "You do not actually believe Gavgal would be so careless with a magical weapon, do you? I had no choice. He would have led all of us to our deaths. After all, you know the reason our numbers are so small is because he killed them. I was there when he killed our mother and our father. You were too young to remember."

Seth was right. Alax didn't remember. All he remembered were the shrill, distant screams and the servant girl who had carried him into a closet to hide. Finally, Alax asked, "What about Morvack?"

"What about him? Had he stayed, had he listened to me, he would not have had to betray us. He felt he had no choice. His response to what you now know was to leave us in favor of an Arkeeronish sorceress. Were I in his position, I might have done the same. Morvack was always so… emotional."

Alax was surprised by the warmth in Seth's voice when he talked about Morvack. "You seemed so angry with him."

"I am. I do not like being dismissed so easily and losing to an Arkeeronish whore. We're his brothers! Blood. Don't worry. By the time we put my plan into action, he will either come back to us with his Arkeeronish sorceress, or he will die with them. That is his choice to make. Never mind him. We must concentrate on the weapon for now."

Alax watched as Seth turned his attention back to his books. He was not interested in the weapon now. Instead, he wanted to be alone. The idea that his eldest brother, now thankfully dead, had killed his parents and lied to him, made him queasy. He had to find a way to make sense of the world again, if that were possible. "Actually, I am not feeling well. Do you mind if I go to my room to lay down?"

Seth looked up again and forced a smile. He had taken on an overly philosophical disposition after hours spent reading about the ways of sorcery. "Of course not. I can imagine how difficult this is for you. You need time to adjust to the truth."

Alax retreated to his small room, closing the door behind him. Throbbing confusion twisted through his mind. Unanswered questions plagued him. Even if Seth did convert to the old religion, it wouldn't change him. It did not change Seth's plans of wanting to be The Emperor of the West Ocean Mainlands. Even with Alax's powers of persuasion, even if he could get it to work on other sorcerers, it wouldn't change the reality that they were clearly outnumbered. Even if they were adept in sorcery, with magical weapons in excess, how could they fight hundreds, perhaps even thousands, of sorcerers who would be against them? There was no possible way they could convince other mages, young or old, to follow Seth. Anyone with an ounce of intuition knew that Seth had no allegiance to the people, let alone to Alax. Seth was only out for himself.

Suddenly it dawned on Alax the true reason Morvack had changed his allegiances. Morvack was tired of being on the losing side. While Alax believed Seth could easily take Arkeereon with their small population of no more than eighty sorcerers, Danaria was different. Not only were they aligned with the Angorans, but they were formidable warriors and trained. Their sorcerer army would be highly adept, unlike he and Seth, and immune to Alax's gifts. But he did not dare share his fears.

Seth would surely lose his temper and become angry, possibly killing him. Alax had no place to go. Arkeereon would be destroyed and the Danarians were not as trusting of outsiders. They would not allow a converted Kersian into their homeland, not that Alax would ever convert, but he might pretend just to save his own skin. He chuckled at his own naivete. It was too dangerous. No. Alax had no choice. He had to stay and weather the coming storm. He soothed himself with the idea that perhaps he would break away to the winning side in the end just like Morvack had done. Deep down he knew that that would never happen. This was an end game. It was him and Seth together to the final battle. With Seth unable to listen to reason, it was all or nothing.

The chaos of these thoughts finally took its toll on him. Thankfully, he fell into a deep sleep without dreams or questions; instead, only the solitude and peace that came with darkness.

CHAPTER 7

Something from a dream caused Aithian to wake in a cold sweat. He sat up and looked around. The room stood dark, and the holding beyond silent. Always, he thought of her. Her image sat just beneath the surface of his every thought and feeling. While he'd lusted after plenty of women, nothing compared to the feelings he felt for Tnasha. Now, he could feel her. She was so close. He shook his head, wondering if the feeling had been sparked by a dream, or his need to be nearer to her. It was no use trying to shake it, for the feeling grew and kept growing with each moment, each breath.

Sliding out of bed, he quickly dressed and padded barefoot into the corridor beyond his chamber door. In the dead of night, he followed his instincts, somehow knowing that they would lead him to her. Finally, in the far southern wing of the holding, he stopped in front of a door of a room he knew should have been empty. Her essence, the vibration of her mana, hung thick in the air. With a trembling hand, he reached out and took hold of the door handle, turning it with a sharp click. The door opened. There, sleeping silently upon the bed, lay Tnasha. His breath caught in his throat. Even though he could not see her, he felt awed by the beauty of her violet outline in the darkness.

He stepped into the room, closing the door gently behind him. There, beside her, he sat in a chair and closed his eyes. For the first time in weeks, he knew he could sleep peacefully.

***

Tnasha woke, cold and in darkness. She shook off the chill, bringing the blanket to her shoulders. After wiping the sleep from her eyes, she looked around and realized for the first time that she was not in her own room. The hard bed beneath her was not her own. Beside her, sleeping uncomfortably in a wooden chair, sat Aithian.

She rested her head back on the pillow, still weak and listless from the mana paralysis, watching his deep blue mana move counter-clockwise around his tall, muscular frame. The cold of the room subsided as a rush of warmth flooded over her. She felt safe here. Then they were kissing, his lips pressed hard against hers, their bodies so close she could feel his warmth. Then the dream changed, and she found herself next to a river where she sat beside Aithian, watching the fast-moving water flow past them on its way to the ocean.

"Step into eternity!" came the woman's voice from directly ahead of her. Tnasha opened her eyes wide, only to find her pupils assaulted by bright morning light.

"Put it out!" Tnasha clenched her eyes shut, half expecting Shanalyn to tell her the light wasn't *that* bright.

"Put what out?" the woman asked. It wasn't Shanalyn's voice.

"The light." The sound of ceramic dishes clanking together rang harsh in her ears. She pulled the blanket up over her head.

"I cannot turn out the sun, but I can draw the curtains," the woman said with quiet countenance.

"Do something," she said, her voice muffled through the quilt covering her. She inhaled, cringing when the scent of musty earth entered her nostrils. Pushing back the blankets, she lifted her arm to shield her eyes. The fogginess of dreaming had left her with the stark realization that this was real.

"You must eat."

"What about him?" She motioned toward the chair, still squinting even though the room now stood bathed in dim gray light.

"Who?"

For the first time, Tnasha opened her eyes. Now fully awake, she looked around. The room was empty except for the small, dark-haired woman standing before her. "Lady Unsere?" Tnasha recognized her.

"Yes."

"Am I…"

"Yes. You are in Arkeereon."

"How?" Tnasha stretched her mind around the question, unable to fathom an answer.

A deep sigh emerged from Unsere's lips. "I wish you would ask my husband."

"Lord Natyis?" It slowly dawned on her what Unsere was saying. She'd been abducted straight from her bed, but how? With a calm expression, she tried to not show her true feelings. Fear. Anger.

"That would be him." Unsere, unable to meet Tnasha's gaze, lifted the covers from the plates of food on the platter that now sat on a small table next to the bed.

Tnasha sat up carefully, still exhausted, and stretched, being sure not to show any emotion. "I thought I saw Aithian sitting here last night."

"That is possible, though I doubt he was directly involved in your abduction." Unsere still didn't meet Tnasha's gaze.

A laugh tumbled, unexpectedly, from the back of Tnasha's throat. "Abducted?"

"Here. Eat." She handed Tnasha a linen napkin.

Tnasha picked up a thick slice of bacon and took a bite, noting Unsere did not answer her question. "I've been abducted?" she asked again. She'd sensed something amiss the first time she'd met Natyis and surmised that maybe he'd been planning this since then. *But then why hadn't he just asked if she would come back?* She wondered.

Unsere finally looked her in the eye. "You find that unbelievable?"

"Yes, I do. I mean," she fumbled for a moment, trying to choose the right words. It was clear Unsere did not agree with her husband, but Tnasha had to find out why. "I sensed something in the way he looked at me the first time I met him, but not this."

Unsere shook her head and sat down in the chair where Aithian had been the night before. "My husband seems to think he has good reason." Then she motioned to Tnasha's mana. "I see his plan of neutralizing your mana did not work."

Tnasha examined her arms and the mana that encircled them. The thin white light that surrounded it the night before, or that she'd dreamed had been there, was now gone and her violet mana moved freely. "He neutralized my mana?"

"Evidently not." Sadly, the matriarch shook her head and let out a forlorn sigh.

"Does he realize how angry my family will be if, no - when they find out?" Tnasha pondered the answer to that question, too, because she wasn't entirely sure how her family would react. By now they must have realized she was gone and she imagined her father, flushed with anger, ordering soldiers to search for her in vain.

"I told him that," Unsere said quietly.

"And he didn't listen." She let out a heavy sigh.

Unsere's mouth contorted into a grim line. "Obviously not."

Tnasha studied the stern expression covering Unsere's face. While Tnasha wasn't thrilled with her situation, Unsere appeared more disturbed about the abduction than Tnasha herself. "Well, you said he must have a good reason?"

Unsere lifted a wary eyebrow and sighed again. "Well… Not really. I don't know, maybe…"

"Oh." Tnasha greedily took another piece of bacon and shoved it into her mouth. It was crisp and warm, salty, and seemed to satiate her growling stomach. Shanalyn had warned her that hunger would hit her once her mana had fully repaired itself.

"Oh? That is all you have to say?" Unsere gave her a pleading look, as if by reacting differently, Tnasha could have changed her situation.

Tnasha shrugged. She was still too weak to plan a grand escape. "There isn't much I can do about it now. I can't use my mana for a few more weeks anyway. I was in mana paralysis until yesterday."

Unsere's brows shot skyward, harshening her soft features. "From what, my dear? Are you all right?"

"One of the sorcerer Seth's mana blates." With a spoon, Tnasha scooped part of a fried egg into her mouth.

A small, appreciative smile made its way across Unsere's lips. "At least you're eating."

"I'm starving, and I'm tired." She felt the fatigue already settling in her arms and hands from the mere act of feeding herself.

Unsere reached out and squeezed Tnasha's shoulder with a reassuring smile. "When you are done eating, I will leave so you can sleep."

In one last feeble attempt at trying to learn more about why she was here, Tnasha said, "The seeress of the Temple Dagon will know where I am, you know."

"I was hoping you might cooperate to avoid a conflict, despite my own disagreement with my husband's rash decision to bring you here." Unsere let out a small sigh.

Tnasha tipped her head to one side thoughtfully. "I might be able to do that, provided he'll tell me why I'm here."

A look of hope washed over the older woman's face. "Then perhaps you could talk some sense into him."

"Would you let him know I'd like to see him?" Even as she said it, a yawn escaped her lips.

Unsere hesitated, drawing her arms across her chest and shifting uncomfortably from one foot to another. "I will, but you should sleep first."

"I'll find out eventually." She sat up straighter and stretched her arms, then used every ounce of energy she had to shovel more food into her aching stomach.

Unsere paused, unsure, then said, "Our family bloodlines are dying. The mortality rate for female children is high."

Tnasha set the spoon down. "Not again."

The hierarch sorcerer's wife looked down in obvious shame at her husband's misdeed.

"What happened to traditional negotiations and arranged marriages? Priestess Caitlan has been advocating selective breeding through arranged marriages for years in order to sustain our bloodlines." This time, there was a hint of irritation in Tnasha's voice and she made no move to remove it.

Unsere shook her head. "He assumed your families would have declined."

Tnasha sighed. "He's probably right. Though with the state of things…"

"Why?"

"It would take years for our family elders to build a trusting relationship like that. The Kersians have definitively destroyed the elders' ability to trust outsiders." She took a long drink of mead and set the half-empty cup down, content that her thirst was finally quenched. Then she narrowed her eyes at Unsere. There was something not right about all of this, she just couldn't figure out what. Her eyes scanned the room for any sign of the Eagle's Talon, but it was nowhere to be found.

"So perhaps he was right," Unsere said. "He hoped you would agree to be wed to Aithian in hopes it would forge an alliance…"

"I like Aithian well enough, but marriage? That's ridiculous." Tnasha's heart was beating more rapidly now. She looked past Unsere to the door, which opened slowly.

Lord Natyis stepped into the room with Eury and Luithian following close behind. "Are you finished eating?"

Tnasha nodded. "I wasn't expecting to see all of you so soon."

Without a word, Unsere stood, replaced the covers over the now two empty plates, picked up the tray, and left.

Natyis looked her over. "You look tired, but we must talk to you, now. I see I was unable to put your mana at ease."

She kept a straight expression even though her mind was racing through the possible outcomes of such an odd turn of events. "Yes. I understand you want me to give myself willingly to Lord Aithian."

Her statement, or perhaps it was how nonchalantly she said it, shocked them to silence.

"We have just started a war," Aithian said from the doorway.

They turned to him. "Don't panic yet," Natyis said, even though his eyes showed uncertainty.

"We have. I know it. I can feel it." Aithian's gaze traveled to Tnasha. When she met it, he looked down at the floor.

Tnasha drew in a deep breath. "Well, I guess we will have to do something about it, because Arkeereon would not withstand an attack by several legions of Danaria's Sirus Horde."

The men looked at her with questioning eyes. "I'm a soldier, not a lady of leisure, remember?" She gave them a wry smile. She had only been awake and able to move for two days and already she found herself in yet another difficult situation where she was the key in stopping a war.

CHAPTER 8

After a mid-morning bath, Seth retreated to his study. He'd been spending a great deal of time there. Upon the oak table sat those items he'd asked one of his soldiers to gather: a sturdy branch of elmwood, a dark crystal cut from Gavgal's temple walls, and a piece of silver. His gaze traveled over the items one by one. The silver would conduct the mana through the wood and into the crystal to project it. Together, these things would create the smaller, portable mana weapon. If it worked, he would use the smaller version as a template to create a weapon much larger, perhaps the size of a catapult. He would mount the large conductor onto a cart so that it would be mobile. With a weapon of such size, he could attack enemy coastal cities and villages from a ship, and have horses draw it inland for use on larger enemy fortifications. No one could defy him then.

A thin smile covered his lips. He had work to do. Gathering up the items in one hand, he left the palace and strode briskly toward the stables where the blacksmith would assemble the weapon by affixing the silver to one end of the branch, within which the crystal would be set. Then, Seth would perform the ritual to infuse the weapon with the properties necessary for it to direct vast blates of mana. He would make it partial to his mana, to alleviate any threat of another sorcerer using it against him. It was an ingenious plan, indeed.

***

Alax dismounted the bay mare he rode and loosened the girth. Unlike Gavgal and Seth, he cared about their horses. Horses were difficult to come by, and he preferred to keep the same horse as long as possible. Getting to know the horse made riding a pleasure for him. As he entered the stable courtyard leading the mare, he saw Seth standing over the blacksmith, watching him work. It seemed odd, but Alax did not question. He passed Seth with a brief nod and went on to care for the mare. After he removed the saddle from the sweating beast, he wiped her off with a damp rag, and took her for a walk around the courtyard to cool off.

Seth stopped him on his way back to the stable. "Aren't you even the least bit curious what I'm doing?"

Alax shrugged. He noted the smug look on Seth's face. "Should I be?"

"We have stable hands to care for the horses. Hand her off to one of them then come see it." Seth's sly grin made Alax uneasy.

"All right." Alax did as instructed, well aware that any show of emotion could set Seth off.

When he returned to Seth's side, Seth took him by the arm and motioned toward the blacksmith's creation. "Look at it."

Alax fought back the disgusted grin that threatened to emerge. The blacksmith's creation was a pitiful looking thing, but he knew if he smiled, Seth would have no qualms about flogging him. The branch was no more than an inch thick. The crystal was thinner. Both were fixed together with a band of silver. Now, the blacksmith engraved the symbols Seth had drawn for him on a piece of parchment into the silver band. "What is it?"

Seth nudged him and lifted an eyebrow.

"Oh." It did not look like a weapon to Alax. It was only a cubit in length. "It looks… small. I was expecting something longer. It's not even as big as the staves the Arkeeronish created."

"This is only a test, dear brother. If it works, we will build a second. These small ones will be our personal weapons. Then we'll build one much larger."

"And where would we get a larger crystal and that much silver?"

"There are plenty of materials in the temple and palace to fulfill that need. We will have to use a compilation of crystals to create a large one."

"Only if we destroyed the walls of the temple to dig out all the crystals and melted down all the silver in the palace."

"If that is what we must do, then we will."

"That will be a bit sudden. It could shock the people." Alax bit his upper lip, then leaned in toward his brother and in a whisper added, "They do not yet realize you do not subscribe to Gavgal's spiritual beliefs or practices."

A wide grin slid across Seth's face. "You worry too much, Alax. I have the soldiers on my side. They worship the blade. They never saw Gavgal as a God. I suspect they will not question my authority. It's the people who might protest."

"What will you tell them?"

"Not I, brother. You. Perhaps it is time for the Unnamed God to get a name and a pantheon of gods beneath him. A rival pantheon. A new mythology. Perhaps our brother was not worthy to know the truth, but you..." Seth narrowed his eyes. "You could easily convince them the new pantheon speaks to you. Have you been practicing on projecting?"

"I haven't had opportunity to address a large crowd of people," Alax started in protest.

"It's no matter, Alax. When the time comes you can do it. I have faith in you. When I become the ruler of this world, you shall stand beside me. I will put you in charge of communicating with the divine. We should give you a title."

Alax's eyes widened in surprise. Seth giving *him* a title? That was akin to sharing power, something Alax never thought he'd see. Then his reason weighed in. No, Seth wasn't sharing power, he was buying Alax's allegiance with a title. "What would you call me?"

"Sorcerer Prime. It's far grander than *high priest*."

Alax tipped his head to one side, contemplating Seth's offer. True, he had always been a puppet for one of his brothers, used to convince the troops of many things, but he had never had a title, especially not one that suggested the respect and power of *Sorcerer Prime*. On the other side of that, a title was something Seth likely thought he could use to further control Alax. Of course, if he was going to die anyway, perhaps a title wouldn't be such a terrible thing to have for a brief time before that happened.

"It sounds good, eh?" Seth's smile was genuine.

Finally, Alax nodded, giving in to the inevitable. "It sounds like an amicable plan."

Seth gave him a brisk nod. "Meet me in the temple later. We will infuse the weapon with mana there. After the evening meal?"

"I will be there." Alax left the stable courtyard, Seth, the blacksmith, and the weapon behind him, his gut filled with dread and disgust.

Alax had his doubts that such a frail weapon could damage anything.

"It doesn't look like a powerful staff." Alax looked thoughtfully at the length of wood with silver and the crystal affixed to one end.

"Looks can be deceiving. I suspect it would easily be able to knock a person from a horse, cause another sorcerer to lose his breath. Two hits could render a sorcerer unconscious. It may take a little more than one blate to cause death, but you can kill anyone with anything if you know a man's weakness and can use the item to exploit it." Seth opened the leather-covered book that sat on the altar and thumbed through the pages slowly, as if looking for something.

"Do we have to do some sort of ritual to *other* gods?" Alax realized too late that his voice was laden with annoyance.

Seth didn't admonish him though. Instead, he snickered. "Yes. After this is over, I suggest you read these books and attempt to commit them to memory."

Alax didn't want to provoke his brother's ire. It would ruin his entire day, so this time he made sure he spoke in that flat, even tone, he used often with his brother. "Yes, Seth."

"We cannot have a *Sacerdos Veneficius Prime* who knows nothing of his new gods when he claims to speak to them."

"I understand. I will commit the books to memory." Alax had a strong memory, so learning some ancient rituals wouldn't prove too taxing, though admittedly it sounded boring and pointless.

"Good. I have no tongue or taste for religion. I'm a leader. Religion is just a device to keep the people pacified. I am counting on you."

Alax lowered his eyes with the realization that it was just as true today as yesterday - Seth believed in nothing save himself. "I will not fail you."

Seth picked up a hard, white chalky substance and handed it to Alax. "Draw a circle that encompasses the entire altar with enough room inside so that we can stand here."

"On the ground?"

"Yes. On the ground."

Alax did not ask the questions he wanted to ask. Had he asked, he would have inquired as to the reason for the circle. What was it keeping out, or in? He figured he'd learn soon enough once he read the books himself. Instead of questions to be answered later, he did as he was told and focused his full concentration drawing a solid white line on the marble floor of Gavgal's temple. It wasn't working so well. The substance crumbled as he pressed it to the floor, leaving a faint line and pieces of sediment. "Does it have to be solid?"

Seth looked down at the circle and shook his head. "It will have to do. I created the lime according to the recipe in the book, but I probably should have added more oil, so it would stick better."

Alax paused at his brother's long explanation. It was not like Seth to over explain anything. He continued on until he had, more or less, a circle drawn on the temple floor. When he was done, he set the small brick of the left-over chalk back on the altar. "What shall I do now?"

Turning the book facing Alax, Seth set his finger on one of the pages, prompting Alax's gaze to follow. "Read through this. I will anoint us both."

"What is the purpose of the anointing?"

"I don't know. Perhaps once you read all the texts *you* will be able to tell *me*."

Alax felt a strange chill wash over his body. Something about not knowing the purpose behind each action of the ritual made him uncomfortable. He wondered then if he and Seth were delving into something neither of them should have been.

"Stand like this," Seth said, showing him with his palms faced forward and feet slightly apart.

Obeying, Alax did as he was told. Seth placed the oil on each of his wrists, on his temples, between his eyes, and at the base of his throat. In each of those spots, a tingling sensation tickled his skin, then began traveling inward through his body. It was as if the oil itself was moving through Alax's mana.

Alax's face must not have masked the surprise and anxiety he felt at this sensation because Seth gave him a strange look, and said, "It must be working."

Alax almost asked him what was in the oil but thought better of it and bit his tongue. It was another thing the books would teach him. His gaze followed Seth to the other side of the altar, tracking his movements. Then his eyes fell to the pages of the open book. "You have to anoint the wand now."

"Yes." Seth did this.

"The oil must conduct the mana from us to the object."

"Perhaps we should just do it and analyze it later. Hmm?" Seth shot him an annoyed look.

Alax clamped his jaw shut and looked on as Seth anointed the wand, then set it in the very center of the altar. Both men held their arms in front of them, palms facing the wand, outstretched. Quickly, Alax's eyes scanned the incantation upon the page. Undoubtedly Seth already had it memorized. He read it several times, well aware that Seth was waiting on him.

Together, they intoned the incantation in perfect unison. "We draw upon the old gods. Come forth! Infuse this tool with our power, but let no others wield it. Subquedor."

After they had repeated the words several times, the wand began to glow a vibrant crimson streaked with yellows and greens. Finally, the color solidified, and the object took on a luminescent color of its own, a dark maroon with a band of semi-opaque white mana encircling it. Both of them took hold of it, Seth on one end, Alax on the other, balancing the wand to their own mana.

Alax looked up, meeting Seth's hardened stare. "It is done?"

Without expression, Seth answered in repetition. "It is done." He pulled the wand from Alax's grasp, lifting it up in front of him. "Let's test it."

"Here?" Alax became suddenly aware of the fear in his own voice.

"You act as if we're children doing something we shouldn't. Bring the book and the oil. We'll go to *the grove* where it's secluded, and we shouldn't be disturbed." Seth began walking, giving Alax no choice but to follow.

Alax knew *the grove* well. They both did. It was where they played as children. The path was still the same, and still work-worn. They'd used it a great deal as children and undoubtedly children used it now, for it was too narrow for adults and both men had to pass sideways through some of the underbrush. It took a short time to reach the grove of ancient, twisted oak trees that canopied over a rich undergrowth of bushes and plants with only several outcroppings of exposed rock bare to the dominance of nature. Without warning, Seth held the wand at arm's length, and a blate of mana emerged from its crystalline tip, crashing into one of the rocks in a display of orange sparks.

Alax jumped.

Seth let out an amused snicker. He handed the wand to Alax and took the book and oil from him. "You try it."

Obediently, Alax held the wand at arm's length and forced a blate through it. This time, a larger blate emerged, sending soil and shavings of rock into the air in a small blast. A pervading sense of lightness sifted through Alax's head. He stumbled backward and regained his balance. Feeling Seth's hand on his arm, steadying him, Alax came around, feeling more aware and sick to his stomach. In that moment he realized the gravity of the weapon's power, and his conscience reared its ugly head. *Morvack had a conscience, and I do too,* he thought. That was the problem.

"Do not force the mana unless necessary. Just let it flow. Otherwise, you will weaken yourself. Allow the wand to do the work," said Seth as if he'd been doing this for years.

Once he regained his bearing, Alax handed the wand back to Seth. "It will take more practice."

Seth handed his brother the book and oil again. "It is all within these books. Now that we know it works, we can begin collecting materials for a second, and for the larger weapon."

Together in the darkness, they made their way back to the palace: Seth content in his success, and Alax unsure of his future.

CHAPTER 9

"Then you will say you came here willingly?" Natyis' expression begged for an immediate answer.

Tnasha let out a sigh, knowing that whatever she said could have profound effects on the outcome of her current situation, especially since she was still in no position to use sorcery as an escape. "I will say whatever it takes to avert a war, but only because I believe we all make mistakes and do things we're not proud of."

"I do not believe I made a mistake. I believe you know I'm right. You may have made the same decision in my position." Again, there was something he was holding back, Tnasha could feel it.

Her eyes widened in surprise. "Would I?" She contemplated what he said for a moment, then shook her head. "No, I probably would have written a letter offering friendship, or visited Danaria myself and told the Council of Elders the truth. But then I know them, and your reasoning would have weighed heavily on their decision. Perhaps it would make sense to them."

"Now what?" Natyis looked around the room expectantly.

"I am going to get more rest. I am still recovering from mana paralysis. You can do whatever you usually do." She clamped her jaw shut, painfully aware that she had just subtly dismissed Arkeereon's head elder of the Imperial Hierarchy.

An amused smiled crossed Aithian's lips, then quickly vanished.

Taken aback, and without a word, Natyis stood. "Then we shall allow you to rest and discuss it more once you're feeling better."

Luithian and Eury followed.

The only one who remained was Aithian. Once the elders had gone he finally spoke. "I apologize for my elders and their rash decisions. I was only made aware of their inane plan yesterday and disagreed with it. I was hoping we could meet again under more favorable circumstances."

She smiled up at him, but in her heart, she felt confusion. Initially, there burned a warmth in her chest from her heart's rapid beat, yet in her mind, she fought to maintain that warrior image she'd worked so hard to attain. "I am glad to know that kidnapping unsuspecting women is not something you're comfortable with."

"I will leave you to your rest." He turned to leave, then paused. "You can leave this room. You do not have to stay here."

"Then perhaps later you will take me for a walk outside?" Though she was tired, a flush of crimson made its way into her cheeks.

"Yes, if you wish," he said. The door closed gently behind him as he left.

Tnasha buried her head in her hands. She felt helpless and stupid, realizing this was how her cousin Margore probably felt when he was around Lady Brianna. Flirting was still foreign to her, and now she felt unsure of herself. This was certainly no time for insecurity, let alone frivolity and behaving like a naïve, love-struck girl. Exasperated, she fell back into the bed and pulled the thick, warm quilt up over her head.

***

Late afternoon brought Aithian back to her room. She felt him moments before he knocked roughly on the door. Weary, but excited, she sat up and swung her legs over the side of the bed, glancing down briefly to make sure her clothing was in proper order. Her heart started beating more rapidly, something she noticed happened each time she came in contact with him. "Come in."

Aithian entered the room, glancing around as if to make sure they were alone.

A yawn escaped Tnasha's lips and she lifted a hand to cover it. She didn't want him to think she was too tired for his visit. "Is it already afternoon?"

"Yes."

She tried to stand, feeling weakness slide up her calves and into her hips, causing her to sit back down. It was no use, she was still much too tired.

He started toward her. "You are still weak from your mana paralysis."

She nodded. "But I still want to go for a walk."

He took a robe from the chair and approached her, holding out his arm. "I'll help you. If you become too tired, we can come back."

She stood again, grasping his arm for support, and took the robe from him, wrapping herself inside it and securing it closed with the belt. Taking his arm, she leaned into him, allowing him to help her from the room. "It seems strange," she finally said as they walked through the sun-drenched the corridor.

"What?"

She shifted uneasily. "The last time we saw each other we were trying to get away from Kersian sorcerers together, and now here we are. I'm your prisoner."

He pursed his lips. "You mean Lord Natyis' prisoner."

She caught the edge in his voice and looked up at him. "I didn't mean it *that* way."

His jaw visibly relaxed. "You don't understand how little my protest meant to him. Were it my choice…"

Tnasha squeezed his arm. "I know. I'm sorry. It's just that I know my people. They will see it as an act of war. Not to mention I'm not happy about being here under these circumstances."

In a way, it was her own fault. She never shared with her father, or Shanalyn, or Caitlan, or anyone her thoughts about Aithian. Or the imperial hierarchy. Even if she sent them a note telling them that she chose to come, her father would believe she was forced to say it. Her father knew that in her present condition, Tnasha's mana was not strong enough to teleport her anywhere, even under anomalous circumstances. He would know she had been taken and there would be doubts. She looked up at Aithian again.

He sighed heavily as if he knew her concerns. After a few more paces, he stopped. "They are not going to believe anything you tell them, are they?"

"No," she said in a whisper. "That's the price I pay for being a private person."

"There must be a way to convince them…"

She let out an insincere laugh. "They wouldn't believe that you and I were in love. Nor that I would want marriage or a family. You do realize that I am a soldier, right?"

"So you keep saying. Would those things be so unbelievable?"

She pulled away from him. "If you knew me better - yes. You don't understand. I am not ready for marriage and a family. I've never had interest in either." With each word, her voice grew in pitch and strength, and she felt tears come to her eyes. "I was perfectly happy with my life until the Kersians ruined everything. Then I meet you, and Natyis took advantage of my feelings, as fleeting as they were, and decided to make things more difficult!"

Aithian reached out toward her, his face pale and his eyes filled with worry. "Calm down."

"You're not the one who has been taken from your bed in the dead of night!"

He looked down at his feet in obvious shame. "I'm sorry for what Lord Natyis did. If I thought I could have stopped him, I would have."

She drew in a ragged breath, fighting back the tears of anger that came with lucidity and the realization that she felt violated and trapped. "You didn't try hard enough. Had you, you could have stopped him."

With a pained look, Aithian tried to pull her closer. "You're right. What can I do?"

"There's nothing we can do." Resignation filled her voice and she wiped the dampness from her eyes.

"Would it make a difference if…" he paused as if searching for the words, then winced as he said them. "If I told you I love you?"

Panic and fear ripped through her chest. She turned from him.

She felt his hands on her shoulders. In a soft voice, he said into her ear, "Why do you put up a wall between yourself and the rest of the world?"

"Because the world is a horrible place."

"It doesn't have to be."

"Only if you're naïve and blind." She turned back to him, shaking. "Even if I did feel something for you, it wouldn't matter. No one would believe it."

His voice softened. "I would."

She didn't want to talk about it anymore. "I'm tired."

"You're avoiding your feelings for me."

Her face went hard. "What do you expect me to do? Sit back and pretend everything is fine? That you and I can marry and live happily ever after?"

"Let's go outside." He gently took her by the arm and helped her outside, into a warm, sunny courtyard. The holding walls stood high above them, but the space was wide and sunlight streamed into it, showing off the colors of the spring flowers blooming in freshly planted beds. They approached a stone bench and sat.

Tnasha wrung her hands and looked into his deep blue eyes. "I do have feelings for you, but love is something I can't afford right now. I don't even know if I know what love is. What I do understand is that Seth and Alax are still out there. My people will soon wage war on yours. The world is a terrible place."

"You cannot save the world, Tnasha."

She snorted. "You're not the first person to tell me that."

"Then why don't you listen? What are you protecting yourself from?" His eyes pleaded for an answer.

She knew that just any answer would not pacify him. It would have to be well thought and backed by reason and solid logic. Nothing came to her.

He took her small hand between his palms. "Be honest in your feelings and allow them to surface. It won't hurt you."

One of her father's many lectures ran through her thoughts: *A warrior's guise, a leader's guise, is solid, unfaltering, and rigid. You must never show emotion lest you show your adversary your weakness.* She realized then that she had already failed. Aithian did know her weakness. He knew that she loved him. "I have to be strong."

His brows lifted. "For what?"

"For everything that is to come." She didn't bother explaining further.

Aithian shrugged, then said hopefully, "The strength of two together is much stronger than the strength of one alone."

She looked away.

As if he could read her mind, he said, "I'm not your enemy, Tnasha. I'm your friend, but I would like to be more than that."

"I'm not ready." The harshness of her own words rang loud in her ears.

"Then I will wait," he said gently.

A look of worry crossed her brow, and she turned to him. "What if I'm never ready? Not just for a relationship, but what if I'm not ready to face events to come? The Kersians will come back..."

"Sometimes change takes time. Other times it is forced on us. We resist force; it's in our nature." His grasp on her hand tightened ever so slightly. Reassured by his touch, she didn't flinch away when he leaned forward. "I have failed you. But I will not do it again. I will tell Natyis to send you back immediately."

The depth of caring that filled his eyes took her off guard, and for a moment she couldn't help but wonder what it would be like to be with him. Would she ever be able to have a life like that? But her stubborn nature surged up, squashing the feeling and leaving a forcible rush of determination and independence in its wake. She nodded.

He looked out over the garden. "I probably won't see you again for some time."

She watched him, noting the sadness that filled his eyes. Forcing a smile, she moved closer to him and put her head on his shoulder. She had to say it or she would never forgive herself, but she knew she would regret it. "I'm confused, and afraid."

Putting his arm around her, he drew her nearer to him and gently kissed her forehead. "So am I."

You have to be brave, Tnasha, she thought. It was unlikely that, even if he tried, Aithian would not be able to convince Natyis to send her back. Natyis was a desperate man. Whatever he'd seen in his visions had caused him to kidnap her. Deep down, she knew that ignoring the seer's instinct, even if his actions were rash, was likely not wise. Swallowing her pride and fear she said, "I'll write the letter."

"What? But…"

She lifted a hand to stop his protest. "Not because I agree with Natyis' actions, but because he's a seer."

Confusion passed over Aithian's face and he absently scratched his dark head of hair. "I don't understand."

"What would drive a seer to do something rash? He doesn't strike me as someone to make rash decisions." She thought back to Unsere, who had clearly been disturbed by Natyis' actions. If his wife was aghast by something like that, then something was amiss.

Aithian shook his head, "No, usually not."

"Then he saw something." She nodded absently, her eyes distant.

"Yes, you and I together, apparently," Aithian said, half under his breath.

"He's not sharing everything," she said, then added, "Get me paper, ink, and a quill quickly before I change my mind."

Even though she felt a knot in her stomach the entire time she penned it, something - perhaps instinct - told her she was right to do it.

CHAPTER 10

"**I** want every inch of the grounds checked and then I want the whole of Danaria searched!" Termark O'Schoitt could not mask the worry that covered his weathered, aging face. In the past few months alone, Tnasha had caused him more sleepless nights than most fathers with only a daughter ever had. Frightening thoughts ran through his mind. Any number of things could have happened. What concerned him most was that none of the soldiers had seen her leave the castle. She had disappeared from her own room in the dead of night. Something else was missing from the room, too. The staff.

He drew in a deep breath, unaware that he was pacing.

"You are going to wear the floor if you keep that up."

Turning, he noticed his brother, Drazen, two years younger and a foot shorter, standing in the doorway. "You have the entire Sirus Horde searching for her. General Dax is being patient because he is concerned, too. But it won't be long before he calls his men back to their regular duties. He will have no choice."

"Why aren't you looking?"

"Why aren't you looking?" Drazen repeated back to him.

Termark forced a half grin. "I deserved that."

"She is stubborn and strange, my niece." Drazen's gaze went to the window on the far side of the room and went distant.

"Yes, and she's missing," Termark said, trying to get his brother's attention back on the crux of the matter.

"But we both know she has a habit of wandering off and getting into trouble." Drazen's voice rang with hope.

Termark shook his head. "No. She would not have gotten far being as weak as she is. You know as well as I do, Drazen, she was taken."

His brother drew in a deep breath and let it out in a heavy sigh. "Fine, but by whom?"

"I don't know. If I did…"

Drazen cut him off. "Have you asked the Seeress?"

Termark cocked his head and lifted an eyebrow. He'd been so worried and anxious that the Seeress was the furthest thing from his mind. "I hadn't thought of that."

"It's a good thing I did. Amy will be here soon." Drazen's voice was soothing.

Termark breathed a sigh of relief. "What would I do without you?"

"You would manage." Drazen put a hand on his brother's shoulder. "Don't worry. We'll find her, but when we do, we are putting her under full-time, heavy guard."

Termark smiled, imagining Tnasha's protest. "Yes," he finally agreed.

***

Amy sat in the sitting room, the family O'Schoitt surrounding her. She closed her eyes, what little good it did. Behind the whites of her pupils, she saw nothing anyway. It was her natural gift for sense, using her mana, that she made her way in the world. She had been in Tnasha's room earlier and had sensed the remnants of sorcery used to pull Tnasha through a portal. "There were three men. The one who did this, though - he does not mean her harm," she said.

"Who?" Termark's voice was almost a growl.

"The sorcerer who took her through the rift. With the staff."

"Who is he?" he asked again.

Amy opened her eyes and turned toward his voice. "I do not know. He's older."

"Kersians?"

She sensed a sudden surge of uneasiness in the room. "No. He means her no harm. He is trying to survive, but not for himself. For others. He's worried."

Tnasha's mother was the one who spoke. "You are making no sense. Damn seers and your archaic tongues. How can we find her if we don't know where she is or who has her?"

"She is surrounded and safe. There is a man there who loves her." Amy's brow furrowed as her vision cleared. In her mind's eye, she saw a large blaze of fire in hues of angry red and orange. Screaming and crying echoed in her mind. She drew back and pulled her hands to her temples. "Tnasha is safe for now, but something terrible is coming. I sense it."

"Where is she? You must find out - we have no other hope." Tnasha's mother took Termark's hand into her own.

A single word fell from the seeress' lips, unbidden. "Arkeereon."

With that, she heard the clank of chain-mail and the leather-clad boots of men, warriors, retreat from the room in a whirl of voices and growls. At that moment, Amy gasped, trying to call them back, but her vocal cords stood paralyzed against it. For whatever reason, their reaction did not feel right. Instead, it felt wrong, very wrong. There was more to the vision, and she was at a loss to interpret it, or explain why she could not see beyond the fire and screaming. Nor could she see beyond Arkeereon. Inadvertently, she had started a war.

***

It was the first time in years the Danarians had waged war on anyone other than the Kersians. After the message had been delivered, mysteriously at that, Warlord Termark O'Schoitt weighed the situation heavily. The note from his daughter had arrived less than an hour after they'd spoken to the seeress. It said Tnasha had gone to Arkeereon to meet with friends, and that there she had found a man she wanted to spend time with. He crumpled the note in his fist. Drazen sat in the chair across from him. "You don't believe it?"

"No," Termark said plainly. He smoothed the parchment out on the table and stared at the even forward sweep of Tnasha's neat penmanship. "My daughter is a warrior. She is not easily swayed by emotion. She doesn't *swoon* over men. She was forced to write it. There was *hesitation* in the writing."

"Hesitation?" Drazen narrowed his eyes and leaned forward, trying to see the letter more clearly. "How can you tell?"

"The words she used." He picked up the now uncrumpled note, selecting the passage that made him wary, and began reading aloud. "Listen to this, brother: 'I am well, and there is no need for worry. Lord Natyis and the Imperial Hierarchy are proving to be excellent hosts, as I expected. I suppose you would like to know about Lord Aithian, but I am not sure what to tell you. He is a kind man, and I am smitten with him.' *Smitten?* My daughter would never use such a word! It's a code. A warning that something isn't right."

Drazen held back a smile and subsequent laugh. "I do not see how that is hesitation. She's a young woman. They all act like that at her age."

Termark frowned at his brother. "Follow the sequence of events with me. Indulge me for a moment, brother."

"Very well." Drazen sat back and crossed his arms over his chest.

"So, she went to Arkeereon?" Termark's voice was clipped. "Yes."

He ignored his brother's clipped tone. "She was still recovering from mana paralysis, and yet she went to Arkeereon. For her to have gotten there in one day, she would have needed to use sorcery, right?"

"I suppose," Drazen conceded. The point his brother made was beginning to make sense. Sudden realization and understanding filled Drazen's eyes.

"She could not have used magick without hurting herself. That can only mean one thing..." Termark looked at his brother expectantly.

"Someone else used sorcery to take her to Arkeereon."

"Exactly. And why?"

Drazen shrugged. "I must admit even I don't know."

"My daughter shares everything with me. There was no mention of this man until now? Why not? Because they kidnapped her - that's why. She was forced to write that note. Which, by coincidence, was transported here using sorcery. Do you see where I'm going with this? This is not my daughter's doing."

His brother nodded. "I see."

Without a word, Termark crumpled the note for a second time and threw it into the silent hearth.

"So, what is the plan?" Drazen finally asked.

"We have already declared war upon them. I will have Caitlan use sorcery to send a message stating our terms." Termark's frowned deepened.

"We want her back," Drazen said.

Termark nodded. "Or else we take it further."

"Do you think maybe the Kersians are behind this?"

"No." He shook his head. "Their attacks have been infrequent lately."

"Perhaps they are regrouping. Perhaps they had a hand in this." Drazen drew in a deep breath.

"I doubt it."

Drazen sighed heavily. "Why?"

"Because I do not believe the Kersians would be able to come up with such an elaborate plan. They do not possess the intelligence."

"You underestimate our enemy. One of the rules of war, brother. Never underestimate your enemy." Drazen gave Termark that look, the one that said, *you should know better.*

Irritated, Termark sat down and chewed on his inner cheek. "Have you considered that we have more than one enemy? We just didn't know it until now. Besides, Amy clearly said Arkeereon."

"Yes, she did," Drazen agreed.

"Then why do you suspect the Kersians would be involved?" Termark rubbed at the bridge of his nose. Usually, he tolerated his brother well, but today Drazen was getting on his last nerve. He knew it was only his fear for Tnasha's safety that made him feel this way, so he brushed the annoyance aside.

His brother shook his head. "I just can't imagine, after all these years of silence, that Arkeereon would do such a thing."

"They probably didn't know Tnasha existed until she was sent to their kingdom to find the weapon." *Yes, that was it,* Termark thought. They needed her for some reason.

"I guess that makes sense," Drazen said.

"You guess? Of course, it makes sense. Why are you always so quick to give everyone the benefit of the doubt?"

Drazen smiled. "Why are you always so pragmatic?"

Termark shook his head. "We should start packing. A trip to Arkeereon will take time." Termark stood. A knock sounded on the chamber door. "Come."

Shadon Longbowe, the spy from Sherok, poked his dark head of hair into the room. Behind him, blonde and pale and a stark contrast to the spy, Tnasha's friend Kolgern lingered back.

"Lord Termark," Shadon started formally.

"Shadon, Kolgern. Come in." He beckoned them forward with his hand.

Shadon entered cautiously. "We were told Tnasha has been abducted."

"By Arkeereon, yes." Termark looked over at his brother who was standing to leave.

Shadon scrunched his nose and forehead in confusion. "Why would they do that? They seemed helpful during the last conflict with the Kersians. Friendly. Even ally-like."

This caused Termark to raise an eyebrow. Of course, Shadon and Kolgern would know. They were with Tnasha at the battle in Ramathra. "Who is Lord Aithian?"

"He was one of the Arkeeronish sorcerers. He seemed decent. Very quiet." Shadon scratched his scalp. "He did seem awfully interested in Tnasha, though."

"What man wouldn't be?" Drazen asked. He nodded at both of them. "If we're leaving soon, I should get ready."

Shadon lifted a dark brow. "You're going after her?"

"Would you expect less?" Termark asked.

"I suppose not. I just wonder if perhaps a situation like this would be better solved with negotiation." Shadon turned to Kolgern, who opened his mouth in protest, but closed it again.

Termark started toward the door. "I am negotiating. I am giving them an ultimatum. They will either set my daughter free, or we will forcibly take her back."

"If they are that set on keeping her, they might fight back. This would not be a war for humans. They are sorcerers, and knowledgeable ones at that. They're led by a seer."

Termark paused as if considering Shadon's observation. "You're right. We'll need to bring sorcerers."

Then Shadon asked a question that made the idea seem irresponsible. "Is it safe to send as many sorcerers outside of Danaria, leaving this city open to Kersian attack, Sir? We haven't heard from them in awhile, but my sources suggest they're planning something."

Termark's heart sank, replaced by defeat. "Why do you ask so many questions, Shadon?"

Shadon shrugged. "I only want you to consider what you're doing, your lordship, to make sure you are not acting in haste. Some sorcerers should be left behind to protect the women and children. Men would surely die in a mana war, though. Taking human soldiers to Arkeereon is futile."

Termark said nothing, realizing that in his own anger, he had let emotion surpass his better judgment. "Thank you for your advisement, Shadon. I will take this into consideration."

"If I, if we, can be of further service, please let us know." The look on Shadon's face was hopeful.

Termark sighed. They were two of Tnasha's closest friends and he knew they'd never forgive him if he left them behind. Tnasha would be happy to see them.

"Fine, come." Termark gave the spy a quick nod and strode from the room, all the while feeling like something bad would happen any minute that would shatter all their lives. Shadon paused for a moment, but only a moment before he grabbed Kolgern by the arm, and both men hurried after the warlord.

***

It took four hours and six sorcerers, Angorans all of them, to open the portal to Orana Tulk and usher an army through it.

Once the portal had vanished and they'd made their way to the docks, High Priest Graneck fell into step beside Lord Termark. The warlord hadn't wanted him to come at all until Graneck had threatened to seek the high council's permission. He narrowed his eyes at warlord now, smiling thinly "I can use sorcery to keep them from defiling your daughter." He knew his statement would anger Termark.

"Graneck, you assume too much," Termark said through clenched teeth. He ran a rough, calloused hand through his thick, uneven brown hair then turned to the priest. "What can you do? They may have already…"

Graneck frowned, realizing Termark could not even repeat the offending phrase. "Any male near her would be knocked unconscious and imbalanced. It is the best I could do at this distance."

Orana Tulk stood tall and proud around them. Almost finished in its rebuilding after the Exavian-Kersian attack only months earlier, the city smelled of freshly cut wood. The streets still bore the black scorch from the flames that had devoured the buildings. Termark kicked at a loose cobblestone in the street absentmindedly. One could sense the anger that swelled through him. "Do it."

Graneck nodded in respectful acknowledgment and closed his eyes. Around him, soldiers hurried about, busily gathering supplies that would be loaded onto the warships. But he blocked the noise out. If Graneck did anything well, it was focusing on his intentions, and his intention now was keeping the sorceress from harm. Yet, he had his own motivations. Since he could not get the council of elders or the other members of the priesthood to see things his way, to have the sorceress killed, he wanted her on their side. And he did not want her bred. A child born of a woman with her strength in mana would be a curse - an abomination.

His mind traveled over the ocean inlet that separated Danaria and Arkeereon, past the small kingdom of Cabalia on Arkeereon's borders, and inland to the main city of Arkeereon. His attention finally settled on the holding, or what he imagined it to be, and Tnasha. A vague image of children playing scattered his focus, but he recovered quickly. A door opened, and the blurry silhouette of a man's head emerged. Just as quickly, Graneck's mind surged a black bolt of mana into the shadowy figure. The man dropped. Graneck steadied himself and opened his eyes, meeting the gazes of the assembled men. Termark, Shadon, and Drazen stared back at him, waiting. "It is done. There was only one."

Shadon, the spy, bit his inner lip, his dark eyes jumping from Drazen to Termark waiting for their response. They offered nothing. For a moment, he appeared as though he wanted to say something, but thought better of it.

Graneck gave him a wry smile. He was glad the man had nothing to say, and was even happier that Tnasha's friend Kolgern, had been forced to stay behind with his unit. Together, Shadon and Kogern made him nervous. Shadon alone was far more tolerable.

Shadon narrowed his eyes at the priest. "Were you reading my thoughts? That's a violation…"

"Were you projecting them?" Graneck asked.

Shadon's upper lip curled and he narrowed his eyes. "I don't trust you, Graneck. I wouldn't be surprised if you had something to do with this."

Termark shot Shadon a quizzical look. "By that you mean?"

"He has already sent assassins after her once because he's afraid of her. Perhaps he sold her to the Arkeeronish so they honestly believe she is theirs." Shadon leveled his gaze at Graneck. "I don't think jumping straight into war is a wise idea, because there are too many unknown circumstances. We are not privy to the entire situation. I'm wary about who we should be trusting here."

"I have done no such thing." Graneck's face turned hard. "You spies are all alike. Paranoid."

"With good reason," Shadon said.

Termark spoke out, his voice stood laden with concern. "So you are saying that we could be going to war because of Graneck?"

The Sherokean born spy scratched his forehead. "No. Look. Tnasha seemed to get on well with the Arkeeronish who helped us after Seth took the weapon. I have my doubts that they mean her harm."

"Walk with me, Shadon." Termark's order was not a request.

Shadon followed him without question. Graneck strained to hear the conversation, but it was no use. They were too far away.

CHAPTER 11

Alax, in poor humor, followed his brother into the private study.

Seth beckoned him like an excited child. "Get in here and make sure the door is closed. I don't want any of the servants to overhear us."

Alax did as instructed. "Fine. The door is closed, and no one is in the corridor," he said reassuringly, peering at his brother with cautious eyes. "Why are you so giddy?"

His brother put on a half-cocked smile and sat down in his chair. "Our weapon worked."

Alax nodded. "Yes. I know. I was there."

"Don't you see? For the first time in years, we have Danaria within our grasp."

"We may have Danaria within our grasp, but I am still not sure we can succeed. Their sorcerers are adept. Some of them will escape and live. What if…"

"You're thinking again, Alax." Seth narrowed his eyes. "Don't strain yourself, leave the thinking to me. You are merely my mouthpiece. Everything sounds better when it comes from your mouth. I am overly abrupt."

The bitter taste of disgust filled Alax's mouth. But he held his tongue. Even though Alax sometimes wanted to chastise him, Seth was the *older* brother. Alax, being the youngest, had endured his brothers' dismissal most of his life. "Am I not allowed to warn you of possible outcomes?"

Seth's happiness turned to annoyance and he began to fidget with a quill. "Fine. Tell me your concerns."

Alax realized his brother simply did not want to know the truth. "I was suggesting that there could be the possibility that some Arkeeronish sorcerers could escape the initial attack, warn Danaria, who will, in turn, gather allied support from the Angoran sorcerers. Victory in Arkeereon may not be an accurate measure of what we will face in Danaria." He paused, waiting to see if Seth had anything to interject. Seth said nothing. Alax continued. "Eighty sorcerers in Arkeereon. Hundreds, possibly several thousand in Danaria. We don't know how many sorcerers they have. That is a big difference in numbers. A concentrated blate attack on the weapon could destroy it."

Seth's jaw clamped shut and fury passed through his eyes. "Then perhaps we should enforce the weapon with a shield of some sort." Then he added as an afterthought as if Alax would not understand. "A mana shield to protect it."

"How would we apply it?"

"We would do a ritual to infuse it not only with the mana properties it must have, but also the shield." Seth sat back, obviously pleased with himself for coming up with such a practical plan to put Alax's fears at bay.

Alax nodded. Seth's plan was good, but he knew his brother would not have thought of it had Alax not brought that possibility to his attention. His mind raced, searching for another flaw in the plan. "What about the sorceress? The fifth-gen, Tnasha?"

Seth frowned. "I killed her, did I not?"

"You *thought* you killed Morvack, too. We should consider the possibility she's not dead. If she is, what if there are more?" Alax paused, wondering if he had gone too far.

Seth's grip on the quill tightened. "More fifth gens?"

Alax hurried to explain. "Danaria has been selectively breeding their family lines for generations. It would stand to reason that she was not only one, but one of many."

Seth visibly shuddered and looked around for an outside source for the chill he felt. "She's the only one we have seen. There is no reason to suspect there are any more than the one - and she's dead."

"We cannot be certain of her death, nor certain there are not others."

Seth let out a snort. "If I killed one, I can kill another. No sorcerer will withstand our attack. Besides…" He looked at his brother with forced reassurance. "I've been thinking about this. We must assume the Danarians will send their women away once the war starts, with only a handful of sorcerers for protection. We may want to consider sending additional troops to look for them and round them up. We may also have to be selective of the females we keep. We don't need any like the fifth gen."

Alax felt another surge of uneasiness fill his stomach. "I wish I was as sure as you."

"You worry too much, Alax. Let us have a glass of wine." His jaw remained set. He stood and took a bottle and two goblets from a table near his desk. Once he filled the glasses with the deep amber liquid, he brought the goblets back, handing one to Alax. He lifted his glass. "To victory, brother."

Lifting his glass with a weak gesture, Alax managed a grin. "To victory," he repeated, but he did not mean it.

***

Alax's fears concerned Seth. After Gavgal's sudden demise, Seth had taken the small temple within the palace and turned it into his own private sanctuary: a temple of magick and sorcery. Undoubtedly Gavgal would not have approved. Seth chuckled to himself, imagining his brother Gavgal's reaction had he survived the mana blate from the staff weapon he had taken from the Arkeeronish wastelands. He thought about what Alax said. What if the sorceress had survived the attack from the weapon? Perhaps he was foolish to assume she had perished from a simple blate thrown as a final attempt to stop her from taking the weapon from him.

"If she lives, my brother may have a valid concern," he said aloud to no one.

He shook his head. How foolish he was to be worried. He was the new emperor of Zul and the Kersian people, and he had weapons. Powerful weapons. His gaze traveled over the newly renovated temple. It was not a large room. At the back stood a table that served as his altar. Even Alax had not been allowed in here. The walls were decorated with symbols of the ancient Gods, the one his ancestors had worshipped prior to Gavgal's takeover. His people were once allied with the Danarian and the Arkeeronish sorcerer families alike. *One big, happy family,* he mused.

He wondered then how many of the other sorcerers he and Alax would have to kill. Alax wanted young ones to shape and mold. There was promise in that. If they could allow the young ones to live, he could rightfully claim himself an elder and by the old laws, the laws he assumed the Danarians dutifully lived by, they could not question his authority or leadership. Then the lines of sorcerers could continue on and possibly thrive. Seth bit his lip, debating the idea. He still didn't like it. Leaving the young ones alive could backfire. Eventually one of the youngsters would challenge him for power. If he was going to die by anyone's hand, he preferred it be by a child with his own blood. A kinsman.

But then your family lines would not survive, his reason told him. Mana degeneration. If the bloodlines between he and Alax's eventual children crossed, which it would if they were too selective, none of their progeny would survive. That was the nature of things. Sorcerers were a dying race already. His further elimination of the varying family lines brought that extinction closer.

It was a serious dilemma. He began wringing his hands. Once again, the idea to keep the children, females, and males under the age of thirty, became more lucrative. Few of them could be adept with their sorcery. But then the vision of the fifth-gen sorceress, Tnasha, flooded his memory. She was quite powerful, despite her inept ability to control her mana. Seth smiled. Thinking about her excessive mana brought him a solution. He would have to kill anyone with more mana than he possessed. In the meantime, he would become more adept, and the secrets of sorcery would be kept just that. Secret. He would not allow those he allowed to live to practice it, nor would he allow them the knowledge of how to perfect and hone it. That privilege would only be allowed to a select few. Those he chose, personally.

He sat in the darkened room in front of his altar, within a circle drawn in red upon the floor. With his new plan emerging and only in need of slight refinement, he closed his eyes and eased his mind into meditation. Things were going to work out better than he ever expected. He would be emperor, an elder, and godlike. No one would challenge him as he reshaped the world into a kingdom entirely his.

CHAPTER 12

Aithian woke up when he heard the door to Tnasha's room crack open. A thin beam of light from the torch-lit corridor filled the room. He felt Tnasha's still form next to him and the warmth emanating from her body. She breathed softly. He placed his hand on her shoulder, gently shaking her awake. "It seems your dinner is here."

Tnasha rolled over. Other than the shadow of her blanketed form, he could see her eyes, violet and groggy. "Where?"

He shifted his weight off the quilt covering her so she could sit up. "In the hallway, I think. Someone opened the door."

She yawned. "I didn't think you were still here."

"I slept for awhile. I hope you will explain to whoever comes in that this was completely innocent."

A soft laugh escaped her lips. "They wouldn't believe you?"

"Women only believe other women."

"You say that with such confidence. Why isn't anyone coming in?"

"Maybe they saw me?" he whispered.

Tnasha wrinkled her nose. "I think if that were the case they would have closed the door, don't you?"

Aithian climbed over her with limber grace and, without making a sound, slid to the chair to retrieve his tunic and dagger from where he had left them. His eyes searched the darkness for his sword, but then he quickly remembered he hadn't brought it with him. "By the Gods, I swear," he whispered.

"What's wrong?"

He felt Tnasha standing beside him.

"Stay in here."

"Can I light a candle?"

"Yes, but keep the door closed."

"I am a warrior, remember?"

"You are still weak and unarmed. Stay here. Don't argue with me." He looked back at her small frame, hoping he wasn't being too harsh, but it was for her own good. "I'll be back in a moment. I just want to check the corridor."

Now dressed and armed with a dagger, Aithian crept toward the door and snuck silently into the corridor beyond the dark room.

***

Tnasha lit a candle at her bedside, alert and ready as light filled the room. There was no one here, but then she had expected as much. Rubbing her shoulders, she hurried over to the hearth and threw several logs into its center. Bringing the candle nearer to her, she lit several pieces of kindling from the flame and strategically placed it around the logs, catching fire to the kindling beneath it. She soon knelt before a warm fire.

The door opened with a creak. She jumped. Aithian entered. "Two of the children."

"Oh."

He went to her, lifting her to her feet and pulling her into his arms. "I'm sorry I woke you up. I thought for sure it was one of the women. But, judging how late it seems to be, they were here earlier when we were both sleeping and decided not to wake us."

"Aren't you concerned that maybe they thought something illicit was happening?" She felt the smile on her lips grow broader.

He pulled away and looked down at her with raised eyebrows. "Probably. Unless they realized I was sleeping on top of the quilt while you were beneath it.

Tnasha shook her head and smiled. If this had happened at home in Danaria, she knew exactly how her family - especially her cousin Annetta - might have reacted to such a scene, no matter how innocent. "No. Top of the quilts means nothing. Trust me."

"Maybe I should go." He seemed genuinely nervous now.

"I don't want to be left alone in here. I feel like I'm being imprisoned and exiled to the wing of the holding no one ever visits." She formed her lips into a pout.

"Is it true?" He wore a look of amusement now. "The warrior fen Schoitt has a vulnerable side?"

Tnasha's eyes went mock-wide. "Am I allowed?"

He feigned shock. "What kind of a question is that? Of course, you are."

Without warning, a child's voice came from beneath the door. "Uncle Aithian, will you come out and play?"

Aithian closed his eyes with a resigned sigh. "Rebbi, I'm busy."

The laughter of children rang through the corridor.

Tnasha smiled and rested her head on his chest.

"I'll get rid of them." He turned his head toward the door. Tnasha moved out of the way, and he went to the door, opening it quickly and thrusting his head out with a playful growl, likely expecting four children to scatter.

Instead, Tnasha gasped when something black jumped at him from a single point of light in the wall adjacent the door, striking Aithian in the head. His body stiffened, then dropped with a thud to the floor.

Tnasha's heart pounded in her chest, so loudly she could hear it. She saw the dark sliver of ethereal shadow emerge from his back and dissipate. It was in that moment that she knew the true war had begun. Nothing she could have said, or did, could have stopped it.

Tnasha forgot her own weakness and hurried to his side. Adrenaline fed strength to her legs as she knelt down beside him. Aithian was unconscious but alive - *thank the gods*. She stood and rushed into the empty corridor. Not wanting to leave him, she emptied her mind and focused on finding the others in the holding. "Hurry!" her mind screamed out to them. "The war has started, and Aithian has been injured!"

She paused, listening to the silence for a rush of footsteps, but there was none. Her thoughts flashed to Danaria. Which of her brethren had enough strength to do something so terrible? A plethora of names came to mind and stopped on one. Graneck. First, he had tried to kill her and all he received was a slap on the wrist and harsh tongue lashing from his wife. Now, perhaps he was trying to redeem himself by saving her from Aithian, a man from whom she did not want to be saved. *That ass,* she thought. Tnasha closed her eyes and reached out to see if she could feel whose energy had touched his. There it was, gray and aggressive. She knew it was Graneck.

Aithian moaned from the ground, and she immediately forgot her rival and leaned down to Aithian to see if she could help him. Luckily, the Arkeeronish prince did not appear to be seriously injured, just slightly imbalanced. She could fix that. However, if Graneck persisted, she would have no choice but to retaliate.

A sigh of relief escaped her lips when she heard the footsteps of the other hierarchs coming to help. There was no way she would be able to lift Aithian to the bed by herself.

***

Once Aithian was comfortable and resting, Tnasha turned to Natyis. She imagined her expression must have been threatening for he stepped back from her. "That fool Graneck did this! I'm in my right mind to… Ugh!" She threw her hands up.

Natyis appeared grim. "Who is Graneck?"

"High priest of the Temple Dagon. The one who hired the assassins to kill me while I was searching for the Raven's Claw?" She looked at Natyis expectantly, as if he should have known who she was talking about. She waved her hand. "I'll take care of him when I see him."

Natyis said nothing. Instead, he exchanged glances with the other men present.

"Where is the Eagle's Talon? Bring it to me. I can see them with it." Tnasha sat down heavy in the chair, absently chewing her thumbnail.

The elder nodded to Eury, who disappeared back into the corridor. Then Natyis turned to her. "What now?"

"If I can see their movements and at least know what Graneck is doing, then I can keep everyone safe and keep Graneck from attacking the rest of you. If he was able to hone in on Aithian, that means Shadon or Kolgern are with him and he's probably drawing on their memories to attack. That could mean more of you are in danger. We'll have to do a protection spell."

Eury returned soon enough with the Eagle's Talon and handed it to her. When she took it, the black stone changed color and she felt it vibrate in her hand. She looked deep into the void. Her gaze moved beyond Arkeereon and through the swirling mist within the stone, into the void of space. There, she saw them. The war ships were on their way and she had to stop them.

She drew back and refocused on Natyis and Eury. "They didn't believe my note. I knew they wouldn't. Especially my father. He knows me too well. And had I known it would have helped, I would have mentioned Aithian to him the night before you brought me here. I had the opportunity, but other subjects seemed more dire." A flush of red crept into her cheeks. "My father is not really the type of man you would share your secrets with. Not…"

Natyis nodded in understanding. "My sons might say the same about me." His gaze traveled to Aithian's unconscious body and Luithian and Verrine who sat next to him talking in hushed voices. "Is he going to be all right?"

Verrine nodded toward Tnasha. "If she balances him, he will be fine."

"I'll take care of him. It's my fault anyway." She sighed heavily, feeling weak and vulnerable. That made her even angrier. "Don't worry. If they make it here before I have a stern discussion with them…"

"Before?" Eury asked.

"I intend on broadcasting a loud message the closer they get. They've only reached the port at Orana Tulk. Some of the troops are already aboard the warships, but I doubt my father is there yet. I would have seen him."

"That stone alone helps you see?"

"Of course, it does."

Natyis narrowed his eyes. "The staff is only a tool. It amplifies a gift that is already there. That's not as common a gift as you seem to think. It's not the staff alone granting it."

She went over to the bed, prompting Verrine and Luithian to move out of her way. She handed the staff to Eury. "It seems *I'm* not very common. You do realize that once I regain my strength I could easily vanish from here?"

Natyis shook his head. "You won't."

She sat down on the edge of the bed. "How do you know?"

He smiled. "I see, too. And from what I can see, you have already made up your mind."

She looked down at Aithian, touching his mana, pushing it so that it swirled around him clockwise. "You see right through me."

"No. But it takes very little to see that you do not back down from a challenge. The bigger the challenge, the more stubborn you become." Natyis appeared amused.

"Because I went after the Raven's Claw?"

He drew in a deep breath. "I suspect that was not the first time. I saw you being taken prisoner. Something about saving Rassia? What is Rassia?"

He really did know her secrets. Her back stiffened defensively. "*She* was the daughter of a warlord. I was forced into that situation. I had no choice."

Natyis tipped his chin and lifted a stern eyebrow. "We all have choices, Tnasha. You had a choice."

Once again, she realized she was wearing blinders. Focused and determined, she was not going to let this war happen. Her own family and people would have to kill her first. "You're right. I do have a choice."

CHAPTER 13

Termark looked around to see if anyone could hear them, then said, "I dislike Graneck as much as you. But what you accuse him of is treason. Accusations like that are strong."

Shadon gave the warlord a concerned look. "I was merely pointing out a possibility. I have no proof to back up my claim. But it would not surprise me if he did have intentions of trying to get rid of her in some way."

"Graneck may fear my daughter's abilities, but it would seem to me he would want to keep her close rather than hand that power to someone else." Termark, of course, trusted no one. Not even Shadon, and certainly not Graneck, but he kept his suspicions to himself.

"You are probably right. I am just trying to consider everything. Maybe Tnasha did go of her own free will. My point being that we do not know what has really happened. Running off to war without knowing every detail with intimacy is foolish."

Termark was well aware of the edge to his voice, but the spy was starting to annoy him with his continued suggestions and liberties. "I might agree with you *if* Tnasha were prone to running off, Shadon. My daughter knows better. I would have to approve of any reasonable pair bonding, and she knows that. Other sorcerers would know that. It is the unwritten law of our kind. These men, by taking her, have scorned our traditions and thrown them in our face!"

"Perhaps here in Danaria. With respect, sir, the Arkeeronish have built their own culture and their own unwritten laws and customs. We cannot assume they believe as we do." A strange look passed over Shadon's face, then he asked, "What if they were afraid you would refuse Tnasha's marriage to one of their sorcerers, so they decided to take her? You have to admit that of all the sorcerers left, Danaria's bloodlines are the only ones flourishing right now. You have more women than they do. Perhaps they figured they could take one and no one would notice."

Termark's eyes widened and he felt as though he had been slapped across the face. His words dripped with contempt. "By saying that, you are assuming they think abduction is a reasonable course of action. No civilized man would find abduction reasonable. In that, he would know that taking her would be a risky thing to do. They should have known that. I could not reasonably agree to giving up my daughter to people who refused to contact me through proper channels. I know nothing of them. I will not have my grandchildren raised by people I know nothing of. Nor will I willingly give up on my only child without a fight. She was abducted, and she is a prisoner. That is the crux of it."

"What if they are good pair bond?" Shadon asked.

Termark fought back a groan. "As her father, it is my right to choose a suitable pair bond for her."

"Then again, maybe Tnasha knew that and decided to run away to be with the man she loved. Knowing you would not approve. Is that so hard to believe? She is stubborn, after all." Shadon gave Termark a hopeful look.

A deep rush of fear ran through him because it was possible Shadon was right. He glowered at the spy. "If this is nothing more than my daughter being defiant, then we appear as fools to the Arkeeronish. Warmongers. Then I would wonder why my daughter would hide something so monumental from me. If she were truly in love, I would have consented to meet with the young man."

Shadon nodded.

They stopped at a bench sitting against the side of an inn and Termark sat down, burying his head in his hands. A forlorn sigh escaped his lips. He looked up at Shadon. "I have always been too hard on her. If she is a prisoner, then I did not do my job as her father to protect her. What should I do? I have never been this uncertain. We cannot just leave her there. Nor can we attack a city that may not have done anything wrong."

"I don't have an answer, Sir." Shadon lowered his eyes to the ground, and an uncomfortable silence befell them.

"The ties that bind us as humans and sorcerers are our emotions," Termark said. "I always considered allowing one's emotions to speak for them made that person weak. Yet here I've done just that. I have let emotion outweigh reason."

"In your position, many men would have done the same."

"I have made a fool of myself. We've already come this far." Termark sat back, watching the soldiers moving about their tasks around them.

"And Graneck sent a possibly innocent man into unconsciousness," Shadon reminded him.

Termark threw up his hands. "Yes, and that."

"Maybe your brother would be a better person to talk this over with. I only gather information, Lord Termark."

The warlord looked up at the dark-haired spy, his eyes suddenly alight with hope. "Shadon, you've just given me a perfect idea."

Shadon lifted an eyebrow and tipped his head suspiciously. "What?"

"We will take our warships to Carinth like planned and port them there. Meanwhile, you will go into Arkeereon ahead of us and find out what you can. Send us the information. Better yet, you can get in to see my daughter and find out what has really happened. Graneck can…"

"I wouldn't trust him," Shadon said, interrupting. He nodded toward Graneck, who was watching them from across the square through narrowed eyes, obviously incensed that he had not been invited to their conversation. "He has his own agenda. The bastard's lucky you haven't killed him yet."

"He is the best we have in the ways of sorcery at the moment. He is the only one of us who is able to do anything at a great distance.

We need him." Termark wasn't happy about it, but it wasn't like they had a choice in the matter.

Shadon wasn't going to let it go. "What if the information he feeds you is wrong?"

Termark frowned. "He wants Tnasha back here just as badly as I do. He cannot keep an eye on her power if she isn't here. Regardless, I will threaten his life if I must."

"It better be a good threat."

"If I promise to watch Graneck, you will do it then?"

Shadon scrunched his forehead and let out a deep exhale. "It doesn't feel right, but my feelings aren't what people pay me for. However, if you want me to scout ahead, then I will gladly do so."

Termark forced a grin. "Good. We should get back before we are missed. I will inform my brother and the other officers of the new plan."

Shadon nodded. Together, he and Termark rejoined Graneck, who stood at the back of the cart, in front of the inn, whispering in the ear of Termark's brother, Drazen.

"Subtle attacks will work best with other sorcerers. Coming at them head-on will only encourage a full-frontal defense," Graneck was saying.

"The attack will only be necessary if the information we gather suggests Tnasha has actually been kidnapped. Even then, we will give them our demands for her freedom first. They may become frightened by the sight of our armies and comply," Termark said.

Drazen started into the inn. "Let's get something to drink and eat."

The others followed him. They found a remote table off in a corner and Termark sat down heavily in an empty chair next to Drazen.

Once they had settled, Termark's brother picked up the conversation with Graneck exactly where they'd left off. "Termark has a good point. If we can solve this conflict with diplomacy and tact, we should." Drazen turned away from Graneck, to Termark. "How are we going to find out?"

Termark patted Shadon firm on the shoulder. "Shadon is going to go ahead of us and request to see Tnasha."

Graneck snorted. "Do you actually think they would allow that?"

"If they wouldn't, then we know they are hostile," Drazen said.

Termark agreed. "Exactly. If he is allowed to speak to her, we know it is her choice. Then I will go in to reason with the foolish girl."

"So now you think she may have done this willingly after Seeress Amy was so sure she had been kidnapped?" Graneck shook his head in disbelief.

Termark felt his jaw tightening again: a frequent side effect when he spoke with Graneck. "I am not dismissing the possibility just yet. Amy is not always right. Tnasha could have been feeding her misinformation."

"That would not be to Tnasha's advantage." Graneck leaned forward, scrunching his forehead. "Once we have Tnasha back here, where she belongs, you best get control of your daughter, Termark O'Schoitt. That girl is reckless and tends to jump into things without heed for consequences. It is not wise to allow a sorceress with her abilities loose without a close watch."

"And if I don't?" Termark leaned toward him, making no move to hide the sword he carried.

Graneck stood. "If you do not, I will convince the elders and the priesthood that she is a danger to herself and all of us. She will have to be killed." The priest's threat stunned all of them to silence.

While Termark knew Graneck had yet to convince the elders or the priesthood, he also knew the sorcerer's plan would be considered if the elders felt imperiled. Tnasha's spontaneity was becoming more and more dangerous - for everyone. Never mind that it was partially the fault of the priesthood, who kept insisting on sending her on fated quests guided by obscure prophecy. If left unchecked, Tnasha would fall into the trap of doing something wrong that would change their minds. That is what Graneck wanted - a fire - and Termark couldn't help but feel he'd just given the priest the kindling.

CHAPTER 14

Seth looked over the courtyard from the balcony above. Below him, his best artisans labored over the creation of the weapon. In a single day, the base of the cart and shaft of the weapon had been put together. Now, the stone carvers affixed crystals, dug from Gavgal's temple walls, into the metal encasements that would secure them to the wood shaft of what amounted to a blate cannon. The device stood two men high and was as long and wide as a grain cart. A sly grin slid over his face as he inwardly complimented himself on how brilliant he was.

Alax approached his brother from the side, not wanting to startle him. "They have gotten a lot done already."

"I expect it will be done by morning if they work all night."

Noting Seth's clenched jaw and rigid features, Alax could tell his brother was plotting. "Are we in a hurry?"

A low growl emerged from Seth's throat. "I would like to have the weapon tested immediately." Seth turned to him with a rancid smile. "There is no time like the present, brother. We have the means to do this. Does it matter if we do it now or later?"

Alax felt his stomach turn. Later would have been better. He scratched at his unwashed hair. "Do we finally have a concrete plan?"

Seth's firm hand squeezed his brother's shoulder, and his hot breath, smelling of fish and mint, moistened Alax's cheek. "You worry too much Alax. Just remember your new station. Let me do the rest.

You can help by taking a bath." Seth, not a speck of dust on his tunic nor a hair out of place, turned back to the weapon to oversee its creation.

Alax turned and started toward his quarters, fighting the urge to vomit. True, the thought of his new title and the respect it would bestow upon him was some consolation, but Alax knew that Seth was not a thinker. Gavgal had been the devious one, Morvack the follower. Seth was merely arrogant, and Alax, of all his brothers, had always viewed himself as the smart one. He almost laughed at himself. If he was so intelligent, he would be with Morvack now. He would have switched his allegiances and been safe from Seth, who would never change and paid allegiance to no one. Alax wondered then if Seth would have still created the weapon if he weren't around. Or did Alax, in some strange way, encourage him? No, he quickly decided. Seth would do as he pleased and would be content in turning on Alax if he stood in the way.

But there was no way out and Alax had nothing better to do. No dreams or goals of his own. Trying to take over the world sounded exhausting. Alax walked the long corridors, questioning his own existence and trying to feel something. Numb, he searched the paintings and finery of the palace for something that moved him. Nothing stood out. Everything seemed dull and dry. Dead. When Gavgal was alive, Alax had possessed real purpose. Now that he was dead, Alax's purpose had dwindled until he was nothing more than a pawn in his brother's outrageous plan. He felt weak, so stopping his brother was not an option, nor did it interest him. Not really.

Finally, after walking for minutes that seemed like hours, he found himself in the washroom. Closing the door behind him he sat on the bench and pulled a dagger from its sheath on his belt. He looked down at it, turning it over in his hands. It bore the ritual symbol of the one god - a flame with an equal-armed cross at its center. It had been present from Gavgal for a job well done. Gavgal gave Alax responsibilities. Real responsibilities. The One True God demanded sacrifice to appease him. Now that Gavgal was no more, the One True God grew angry.

A lifeless chuckle escaped Alax's lips and echoed, hollow, against the tiled walls. Did he really believe in the One True God? The old religion? Anything? They were on the verge of a change. Destruction. He brought the blade over his left wrist once, watching the crimson streams of blood pour forth from the wound. He cut his wrist again and again, mesmerized at how painless it was, and how the brilliantly crimson-colored liquid was all it took to feed life. With each cut, the pain made him feel again.

The blade, now covered with semi-translucent blood from his own body, his sacrifice, fell from his grasp to the floor. As he reached down to pick it up, he saw the stars of the universe, and found it hard to catch his breath. A chill spread over him and he slid slowly to the stone floor, exhausted. The room was cold, but he could not bring himself to get to his feet to stand, nor could he carry himself to his bed. So there, he slept, oblivious to the afternoon and the sunset, and finally night.

***

Warmth woke him. Alax opened his eyes to the golden glow of the fire in the hearth. The warm quilts covering him were comforting in some way. Becoming more aware, he noticed Seth sitting in the chair near the fire, staring pensively into the flames. He turned when he heard Alax stir.

"You gave us quite a fright." Seth's voice came out cold and crisp, void of emotion.

"Why is that? You should have left me." He lifted his arm from beneath the quilts. The wounds no longer bled. He could tell because the bandages over them were pristine white.

"What were you thinking? Why would you do something like that to yourself?"

For a second, Alax thought he heard concern in Seth's voice. "I..." he stumbled for an answer, but he had none.

"How could you do this to me? You know I need you if I am to be successful." Seth stood, towering above the bed. The lines around his eyes and mouth deepened as he glared down at Alax, turning his face into a cold, hard mask of disappointment.

Alax felt his face twist in disbelief. "Do you ever think of anyone but yourself?"

"I cared enough to not allow you to bleed to death."

"Not allow me to bleed to death? If I choose to take my own life that is my choice. Not yours."

"You are angry that I saved your life?" Seth sat down heavily on the bed next to Alax, and grabbed his brother's chin, forcing Alax to look at him. "I am doing this for both of us so we can have a better life. I have augmented my plan with your advice in mind. Do not *ever* say I only care about myself."

Alax had nothing to say to this and set his jaw.

"Is life so terrible you would want to die?"

"I feel all hope is lost. I no longer know what I believe. I have no purpose. I worry we will fail and die anyway. I would rather die by my own hand rather than my own stupidity." A scowl made its way across Alax's face.

"You are my brother, and I care about you." Seth shook his head. "But in some ways, you remind me of…"

He didn't say it, but Alax heard the thought. *Morvack.*

"You can be too soft. Morvack was too soft."

Alax scoffed. "Like you cared about Morvack?"

Seth's mouth twisted in disgust. "Morvack turned on us. On our family."

"Do you think I am going to turn on you?"

Seth looked down at his brother's bandaged wrist. "Turn on me, no. But abandon your own kin, yes."

Alax didn't have a good argument for that. Suicide was an easy out. "You certainly didn't care about Gavgal…"

Seth groaned. "Gavgal lived a lie. He held all of us under his thumb. Had we ever married he would have killed our women and children at his whim, or in his anger at his own inability to spawn offspring. Would you have wanted your wife raped and murdered by your own brother?" Seth did not wait for an answer. "We couldn't live like that. And had our brother Morvack not been so weak and spineless, he would be here with us now."

There was a long pause, and then Seth drew in a measured breath. "I need you Alax. I need you to believe in me. To stand next to me. If you need purpose - I can give you that. We need to change our lives for the better. We can bring peace to the West Ocean

Mainlands and to the sorcerers. These people, left to their own devices, are warmongering and self-destructive. We are the key to helping them while helping ourselves. Besides, sorcerers are the superior species, are we not? We shouldn't be cast aside. Nor should we allow humans to slaughter us. They should serve us. We are the ruling class."

Seth's lament sounded almost logical. In a strange way, Alax understood Seth's reasoning, or perhaps he was just looking for a purpose. "Your plan is haphazard and changes too much, too often."

"I prefer unrefined. I'm working on it." Seth squeezed his brother's good arm. "And you are a big part of it. If we succeed, you won't want to destroy yourself. If we fail, we go down - together. As brothers."

Alax searched his brother's face for deception and saw none. Seth was right. He could die nameless on a washroom floor, or he could go out in a blaze of glory. It would be better to live on in infamy. "All right, so the revised plan?"

Seth smiled appreciatively. "I have decided we will not be killing sorcerers twenty-five or younger, or those with less mana than you and I. I'm not completely uncivilized."

Alax blinked in surprise, prompting a genuine smile from Seth. He leaned back into the pillow behind him. "Very well."

"If we killed them all except the women, the bloodlines would not be diverse enough to sustain even one family bloodline. I want our children to be the heirs to the new monarchy. That can only happen if our children have other sorcerers to carry on their bloodline and so on. This way we can make sure we do not destroy ourselves. That," Seth said emphatically, "…was the flaw in Gavgal's plan. He has been killing our future generations all because an heir is something he couldn't have. That, brother, is selfish. I always think of how my plans will affect you."

Alax kept his eyes averted to his bandaged arm. He said nothing.

"You aren't going to try to hurt yourself again, are you?"

"If I were, would I honestly tell you?" He snickered.

"I would hope so." Seth reached out and took his brother's hand. "Things will work. You'll see."

Alax pulled his hand away. "*I* won't kill *myself*, no."

Seth rose. "Tomorrow we will load the weapon onto the ship."

"But we haven't done the ritual."

"We will do the ritual as we travel. It's more efficient that way." Seth stood. "Be well brother. I will see you in the morning."

Alax nodded. "Good night, Seth."

"Good night, Alax." When the door closed behind him, Alax pressed his eyes closed, trying to force himself into sleep. He'd made the choice to live, to boldly go into battle and follow Seth's inane plan through to the end. When they were done polishing the deck of a sinking ship, Alax wouldn't kill himself. No - the sorcerers of Danaria would do it for him. When they did, Alax would take as many of them with him as he could.

CHAPTER 15

Aithian opened his eyes and smiled at the vision he beheld. He stood aglow, bathed in her violet light, his mana's own blue hues subdued by the intensity of hers. Tnasha shifted in his gaze and turned to him with an expectant look.

"Good morning," she sang.

"Morning?"

She nodded with a soft smile. "Yes. Morning. Do you remember anything?"

He went over the night before in his mind and continued to watch her. A stream of sunlight came through the window, lighting her beautiful, tired face. "I remember something black."

Tnasha let out a laugh that made the entire world seem brighter.

"What?"

"That's all? Something black?" She shook her head.

His brows furrowed, and a brief panic washed over him. "Should I have remembered something else?"

The smile faded from her face. "I guess I was expecting something more vivid. A vision at least."

The disdain in her voice did not seem directed at Aithian, thankfully. With a nod, he said, "Oh."

"There is probably something you should know." She paused long enough to draw in a deep, measured breath. "It was High Priest

Graneck. If I had an arch enemy, it would be him. I suspect he wants you out of my life so he can keep control of me."

Aithian sat up. All at once a sharp pain shot through his temple, causing him to wince and bring his hands to his head as his vision clouded. "Oh."

He felt her hands on his shoulder, steadying him. "Are you all right? Should I call for Verrine?"

He shook his head. "No. I doubt there's anything the physician could do. I'm just a bit light-headed. I'm sure I'll be fine in a few minutes." He shifted his weight and met her gaze through squinched eyes. "Is Graneck still trying to kill you?"

A snort escaped Tnasha's small, delicate nose. "Not this time. I think he gave up on that. For now, at least."

"What then?"

"He was trying to hurt you, probably on orders from my father and the High Council." She shrugged and let out a deep, forlorn sounding breath.

"Why?" The answer came to him before she could even respond. His head throbbed, and a surge of nausea nearly overwhelmed him at the thought. He eased back down onto the pillow. "Let me guess. I was the one that abducted you."

"Yes, that probably is what they think. You and I both know it isn't your fault." She looked over her shoulder to the door. "It was Natyis' doing. The problem is that my family sees this as an act of war. Clearly, they didn't believe my message."

"Isn't there anyone who would believe you?" He closed his eyes, listening to her confident and melodic voice. The soft lilt in her accent swam to his ears like a song.

"I'm not sure." She paused. "Aithian?"

He heard her, but he felt too weak to respond. Consciousness slipped away, and he faded into a dream realm where her voice became a mere faded echo in the restful darkness.

***

Tnasha sat heavily in the chair at Aithian's bedside and watched as his mana expanded and collapsed in a frantic attempt to heal the imbalance. She should have known he was too exhausted to talk. It would take at least another day before he felt like himself again. Her only consolation was the fact that her mere presence could correct the imbalance and stifle Graneck's magick. For now, at least. She stood from the chair and climbed into the bed alongside him. She still wasn't feeling well herself. Until both of them were better, they really had no choice but to stay here, in this small room, in an almost abandoned part of the holding.

She wasn't sure how long she'd slept, or even how deeply, but the sound of Verrine's boots clicking against the marble tiles of the floor and echoing off the bare walls of the room finally woke her. Through squinted eyes, she watched as Verrine's twin sister, Verrier, entered the room with some logs for the fire and set about tending to the hearth. "Lady Unsere is bringing them stew," Verrier said quietly.

Tnasha yawned, stretched, and rubbed her eyes before opening them completely. Her stomach growled. "Stew?"

Verrine leaned over her to get to Aithian. "How is he doing?"

She shrugged as Aithian's voice emerged barely above a whisper from behind her.

"I want stew, too," he said slowly.

"If you're hungry, that's a good sign." Verrine stood upright and looked down on Tnasha. "You're looking much better. Your mana is strong again."

"I wish my muscles were." Every inch of her felt stiff and her neck was sore.

"You should get out of this room more and take him with you. Three times a day at the very least."

"Why? In here, people bring us our stew," Aithian said with a weak laugh.

Smiling appreciatively, she accepted that his humor wasn't as dark as hers. "Agreed."

Verrine turned from them with a wide grin on his lips. "Laziness does not promote healing."

"Nor does it stop wars," Tnasha added thoughtfully. "I need the Eagle's Talon. If I can use it to see them more clearly, then perhaps I can figure out a way to stop all of this once and for all."

Aithian sat straight up with his hands cupping his head. "You want to use that thing?"

"We have it. I don't see why we shouldn't use it. Besides, everything happens for a reason." All eyes stood fixed on her. "The more I think about it, even in chaos, things work out."

"By divine intervention?" Aithian's voice hinted sarcasm.

"I don't know. Perhaps. Think about it. A prophecy comes about, foretelling the things I must do. I'm not given any clues as to how I am supposed to succeed, but I do. I narrowly escape each time."

Verrine rolled his eyes as any man of science might have. "Prophecy is nonsense. Everything you have done is by your own will and you have succeeded on your own merit. Narrow or not, success is still success."

A wide smile covered Aithian's lips. He waved a hand at Verrine. "Always the practical scientist."

"Prophecy is nothing more than a way to convince young men, or women, to die in old men's wars. It gives them purpose and hope for a future that is uncertain. It's nonsense." Verrine pulled a small glass and and a bottle of something that glowed green from his bag. He poured a small measure of the green liquid into the glass and handed it to Aithian. "Drink this."

Aithian did as he was told, then stood full height and pulled on his tunic.

Tnasha grimaced. She did believe in prophecy and the prophets who prophesied, or at least some of it. "So, you mean to tell me that Kalath, a dear friend who was like a second father to me, would tell me about a prophecy that did not exist just to coerce me to do something?"

Verrine nodded. "Maybe to give you the courage to stand up to the Kersians."

"But to lie…"

"Verrine has a point," Aithian said. "Sometimes we need lies to give us a little push in the right direction."

She narrowed her eyes. "All right. So, if prophecy is nothing more than manipulation, how do you explain things that cannot be explained?"

"Such as?" Verrine lifted an eyebrow and shot a quick smile at Aithian.

"Sorcery." The smugness she felt took over her expression, and she wore it proudly.

The physician let out a chuckle. "Sorcery is the natural science of the universe. It will eventually be explained if our future generations decide to study it. Bark from a tree can decrease pain, most likely due to alchemical properties of that bark and of the body. So surely there is a similar explanation for sorcery."

"So maybe there is that same science for prophecy," she said.

Both men considered her point, but Aithian finally shook his head. "Prophecy cannot be seen or tested. An act of sorcery can be seen in physical manifestation."

"What about seers then?" she challenged. "Seers tell the future all the time and are right. Isn't that the same thing?"

Aithian shrugged. "That can be tested. Either seers are right or they're not. Telling the future is different than prophecy."

"No, it's the exact same thing." Tnasha licked her dry lips and looked around for a glass of water, but Lady Unsere had left no cups or pitchers. Then her eyes fell onto the men. She did not like where the conversation was going. It was no wonder certain people always ignored the seers, even after they'd proven themselves again and again by being right. She just hadn't expected to meet some of those people here. With Natyis being the one to lead them, she fully expected everyone within the holding believed in prophecy. The idea that prophecy was all nonsense challenged the nature of the Gods. "Then what about deity? Is that nonsense, too?"

Aithian exchanged another amused glance with Verrine. "If you look at deity as parts of nature you can witness, as part of the universe, then deity can be proven. However, if deity cannot be witnessed then it lends speculation to deity's existence altogether, doesn't it?"

"I believe in deity as nature." She looked at him over her shoulder with pursed lips, waiting for him to challenge her again.

"Then you have nothing to worry about. It is when you disconnect deity from all that is when reality fades and a person loses himself in a delusion of fantasy." Verrine had poured another dose of the green liquid. This time he handed it to her. "Drink this."

"What is it?" Holding the liquid away from her, she peered into it. Brilliant emerald light shone from within, casting a green glow. She licked her lips again in attempt to moisten her dry mouth.

"Medicine to heal and strengthen." He motioned her to drink.

She sniffed it and wrinkled her nose in disgust. "It smells like burnt licorice root."

"Don't smell it, drink it." Verrine crossed his arms over his chest, waiting.

"Down it fast, like you would strong spirits," Aithian said.

She did, and gagged, thrusting the now empty glass at the middle-aged physician.

Verrine laughed. "I never said the medicine tasted good. We flavored it with licorice root to help the taste."

"Yes, well, that was disgusting." The liquid settled in her stomach, leaving a sharp, bitter taste coating her mouth.

"The stew will get rid of the taste," Verrier said from the doorway.

Verrine took a deep breath and stepped back, then repeated, "Three times a day. Get out of this room and move around."

Aithian nodded and playfully jabbed Tnasha in the arm. "Where is our stew?"

She shrugged. No sooner had the question been asked, Unsere entered with a large platter holding two bowls of steaming stew and a small loaf of bread fresh from the oven. As much as she wanted to eat, Tnasha knew she couldn't let her original idea go. It didn't matter what the others might think about seers. "Lady Unsere, do you think Lord Natyis could come speak to me, and bring with him the Eagle's Talon?"

Unsere smiled with a gentleness that reminded Tnasha of her grandmother. "I will ask him."

With that, the matriarch set the tray on the small table, prompting both Tnasha and Aithian into the chairs around it. Then, greedily, both Tnasha and Aithian took up the spoons and began eating. Once the taste of licorice and medicine had subsided, it was one of the best tasting meals Tnasha had ever eaten, and she felt stronger by the time she'd finished. Strong enough to use the Eagle's Talon to find a way out of this mess.

***

Time seemed to move ever so slowly, and it felt like hours before Natyis finally arrived. As always, trailing behind him was Lord Eury. With him, he carried the Eagle's Talon. Its fragile appearance still awed her each time she saw it. To the untrained eye, it appeared little more than a mere branch with a polished stone affixed to one end.

"May I ask why I have brought this?" His eyes bore into her with a need for answers.

The question did not surprise her. "I want to use it to see what my father is doing. I need to stop this nonsense, unless you want a bristling army at the holding gates."

The silence stood deafening in her ears. It seemed like forever before he answered, shattering the stillness. "You perplex me."

She felt her face contort into a mask of confusion. "Why?"

He sat down on the chair next to the bed. "You have been abducted, and yet you do not want to be saved."

"I still have faith you will let me go willingly. Your actions may have been rash and with good reason, but you are not unreasonable or uncivilized people." She turned to Aithian, who sat next to her on the edge of the bed, staring off into nothing. He did not offer a response as she expected. She reached out to take the staff from Natyis' hand. He let go of it willingly and sat back in the chair. If there was a good reason, as she suspected, he wasn't going to share it. Not yet.

The smooth surface of the staff calmed her. She ran her thumb over it and looked into the polished stone, watching intently as its surface clouded and then lit up as if it possessed its own internal light. The stone glowed gray and she allowed its luminance to enter her. Focusing, she looked deep into the stone, peering into oblivion with a clear mind, seeing nothing and everything at once.

There was a ship. Two ships. No, four. But only three of them were Danarian. Each of the Danarian ships held two legions of

97

soldiers, enough to effectively take Arkeereon down to its knees in forced submission, especially if they had brought more sorcerers than just Graneck. While this concerned her, what concerned Tnasha more was the fourth ship. When she caught a glimpse of the crew, and of their cargo, an unbidden shudder ran through her body. She wanted to hand the staff back to Natyis, but she held on to it, knowing she had to look deeper. While she saw hope on the Danarian warships, what she saw on the Kersian ship frightened her.

She fought back from the depths of the trance the Eagle's Talon had pulled her into, and she handed the staff back to Natyis. A sharp pain shot through her head and she winced.

Aithian was the first to speak. "What did you see?"

She didn't answer at first, instead allowing the images she'd seen to run through her mind so that she could make sense of them. The heavy, black feeling of the vision of the Kersian ship still hung there in her mind's eye. "It seems there is a purpose to everything," she said quietly.

Tnasha didn't explain further. Now she knew what Natyis had seen and understood why he had abducted her. If he hadn't, the Danarians wouldn't have sent the warships and the Imperial Hierarchy of Arkeereon would have never survived the Kersian attack. This wasn't just a coincidence. At least now, she knew they had a chance. The weight of the world fell heavy on her shoulders and she knew she would have to convince her kinsmen the Arkeeronish meant no harm. The problem was, she didn't know how she was going to manage it. As it now stood, the Kersians would be the first to arrive. She stood, ignoring the perplexed looks of the Akeeronish onlookers. "We have maybe a day at most to prepare. We must hurry. Get everyone together. Have them grab what they can carry. We need to evacuate."

CHAPTER 16

"Cabalia could very well warn the Arkeeronish of our arrival," Graneck said.

Shadon snorted in disgust and cracked his knuckles. It seemed all he could do to keep himself from giving the priest a fist in the jaw. "It is not a matter of whether or not Cabalia will choose to warn the Arkeeronish. They will, regardless. They have strong peace treaties and trade agreements in place. They both extend to the other favored nation status. An attack on Arkeereon will be seen as an attack on Cabalia."

Graneck gave him a bored stare. "Cabalia is no match for our armies. No more than Arkeereon is."

"That's not the point." A disgruntled sigh emerged from the spy's chest, but he refrained from further comment.

Termark lifted his hands to quiet them. "We have only come to find out what truly happened, and if Tnasha's return is refused, to give them our demands. My daughter or war. It's as simple as that."

Shadon nodded in defeat. A gut feeling told him it was not *as simple as that*. Uneasiness swept over the room. "I'm going to get some sleep."

He left them to find a cabin below deck, some place quiet where he could rest and think. There had to be a better solution. Surely, he could sneak into Arkeereon to see if Tnasha was all right, but he already knew the answer to that. Tnasha was fine. She could take care of herself. Aside from that, he had met the Arkeeronish. They were not uncivilized people. Only desperate. Desperation drove sane men to commit irrational deeds. Being able to see their perspective didn't help matters. Another sigh erupted unbidden from his lips. He found an empty cabin and settled in. Laying down, he stared up into the darkness. There had to be an easier way. Soon, he found himself drifting.

Thick fog covered the planes. He could not even see a foot's length in front of him. Her voice came at him from beyond the murk. "Shadon, stop this."

His eyes widened, and a cold chill swept down his arms, causing the fine hair to stand on end. "I don't know how to stop it."

"Make them see."

"It's not so simple. Tnasha, did you write the note?" His eyes searched the fog for a shadow or some sign of movement, but it was no use. She remained hidden from him.

"I did." Silence followed the brief rush of cool morning wind. Finally, her voice lifted to his ears. "Tell Graneck that the sorcery he threw at Aithian was a mere annoyance. If he does it again I will be forced to use sorcery of my own."

Shadon smiled. By her defiance, he knew that he was, indeed, talking to Tnasha. "That alone will not solve this problem."

"No. But you might want to tell my father that there are more important things transpiring. Dire situations. At this moment the Kersians are on their way to Arkeereon to test a magical weapon greater than any we have ever seen."

His knees buckled beneath him. "By the gods."

"We must save the Arkeeronish, Shadon. We have to. They are kindred. If they are to survive, we need to help them," Tnasha said. "With a weapon of this magnitude, the Kersians, Seth and Alax, can enslave all of humanity and lay waste to Danaria with their weapon and their human armies. The sorcerers' race will die."

Shadon sat straight up, struggling to open his eyes. A thin film of cold sweat covered his body. His heart thumped wildly in his chest and he realized he had been dreaming. Or was it a dream? Tnasha had many abilities that no one, let alone she, herself, fully understood. Upon finally deciding it had been a dream, but one sent by her, he forced himself to get up despite his lack of lucidity. His knees were still weak. The darkness of the room overwhelmed him and he found himself tripping over the uneven floorboards in his haste. Termark, and even Graneck, as much as Shadon hated the priest, had to know.

He found Termark amongst a small gathering of the leading officers. Termark looked up at his approach. "Are you ill, Shadon?"

Shadon drew his hands to his face. "Do I look that bad?"

Termark turned back to the map unfolded on the crate before him. "You look as though you've seen the dead."

"A prophesy, rather. If we could call it that... It wasn't technically sent from the gods, though I imagine it was by their divine countenance that I saw what I did." His eyes focused on something distant. When he realized the gazes of all those present were on him, he refocused his attention on Termark. "I need to speak with you privately."

The sorcerer-warlord lifted an eyebrow. Shadon winced, struck by Termark's sudden resemblance to Tnasha. Details flooded Shadon's mind, somehow more vivid than they had been during the dream. Termark stood, and both men stepped out of hearing range of the others.

Tnasha's father looked at him with expectation. "So?"

"Do you believe in Tnasha's ability to work various sorceries at her own discretion?"

"Why do you ask? Of course, I do." He snapped his fingers and a small flame appeared in his palm. "I may not have the mana my daughter has, but where do you think she got it from?"

Shadon's eyes went wide at Termark's revelation. He had never considered the warlord had any magical talent despite the sorcerer's blood that ran through his veins.

"Focus, son. What are you trying to tell me?" Termark extinguished the flame by closing his hand into a fist.

He snapped out of his trance. "Because I believe she has just sent me a dire message."

Termark took Shadon's arm and held it tight. "Is she in danger?"

Shadon looked deep into the sorcerer's eyes. "We all are."

"I knew she couldn't have sent the note." He loosened his grip on Shadon's arm and turned from him with a scowl.

"No. She *did* send the note. It is not the Arkeeronish we need to be concerned with."

Termark turned back to him. "If not them, then who or what?"

"The Kersians." Shadon paused long enough to draw in a deep breath. "They have built a magical weapon larger and stronger than any we've ever seen. They can use it to destroy cities." His voice grew even louder, attracting the attention of every soldier within earshot. "They will test it on Arkeereon, then will set about building their armies to eventually bring down Danaria."

Termark's eyes widened and his jaw dropped, but he said nothing.

Shadon continued, lowering his voice again. "Tnasha says we must save the Arkeeronish."

"Save them?" He set his jaw. "They abducted my daughter."

"She did not sound like she'd been abducted to me. Regardless, the fate of Danaria and the rest of the world are at stake here. We can either forgive their misgivings and work together to stop the Kersians, or we can do nothing and allow..."

Graneck's voice sounded from behind him, cutting Shadon off. "When will this occur?"

Shadon's face fell, and he turned to Graneck with a look of disdain. "The Kersians are ahead of us. We will arrive after they do."

"Our only goal is to save Tnasha. In the wrong hands, she is the stronger weapon." Graneck's cold stare blasted through Shadon.

Shadon snorted and rolled his eyes. "I suppose, since you couldn't have her killed, it's in your best interest to be her friend. Too bad she sees right through you."

Graneck's features contorted into a look of disgust. "You obviously don't understand. It seems to me this is a matter for *our* race to deal with. Not yours."

"Without *my* race, you would have no armies." Shadon balled his fists and took a threatening step toward the sorcerer.

Termark lifted his hands. "Stop. We have no time to waste with petty arguments." He sat down on a crate to ponder all that Shadon had told him, his eyes distant. Without really addressing anyone, he said, "That sounds like my daughter's reasoning. But Shadon, you would know best. How strongly do you feel this information is correct?"

Shadon gave the warlord a half-smile, pleased that Termark showed some trust in him. "With my heart, I know it's true. If any of this information is wrong, I will hand my life over to you. You may take it if you wish."

"Hmph." Graneck narrowed his eyes, studying Shadon like a critical buyer at a horse market. "We are going to trust in a human's intuition?"

Termark shrugged. "I know my daughter has grown to trust him. The council trusts him. He has met the Arkeeronish, and he knows my daughter. I must extend my trust to him. Besides, he has pledged me his life. If he is wrong, I can kill him."

At the mention of Shadon's pledge, Graneck smirked. "Fine. But if I were you, I'd keep an eye on him. Spies have a habit of disappearing."

"And you're a sorcerer, Graneck. It should be easy for you to find and kill me." There was bitterness in Shadon's voice, but he didn't care if the priest heard it.

Termark let out a forced chuckle and shot Shadon a brief, knowing glance. "He has a valid point, Graneck."

Shadon smirked back at the sorcerer, then silently prayed that the gods would strike Graneck down for his underhanded deeds. A wave of guilt washed over him almost immediately. Certainly, Graneck could not be trusted, but even Shadon knew that Graneck's deeds were driven by his own fears and imperfections. *Even sorcerers have flaws,* he reminded himself. A snide smile crept across his lips as he thought of Tnasha's imperfection. For a sorceress she seemed more adept with a sword. Sorcery was something she had difficulty controlling, though he had to admit that she was getting better with practice.

He looked up to the sky. The full moon hung there, glowing its white, heavenly light and casting just enough luminance to make the water seem ethereal, almost mystical.

***

Graneck moved off to one side of the deck so he could be alone with his thoughts. How could a human have such dreams? He wondered. Tnasha, of course, his mind reasoned. The priest shuddered at the thought. Her power grew even now, he was sure of it. As unsettling as it was, she was becoming too powerful to control. If she could no longer be controlled, what then? Would her magick grow infinitely? Would any of them be able to stop her? Would her mana implode and kill her? Or would she merely go insane with mana sickness like the Grand High Priestess Anne fen Connacht?

Fifty sorcerers went after Anne, but only after she had killed two elders, four temple priestesses, and eighteen sorcerer warlords including her own brother. Anomalous sorceresses were dangerous, but it seemed the council of elders had forgotten. Or perhaps they were afraid of Warlord O'Schoitt's reaction to such a decision. She was, after all, his only child. "How easily we forget," Graneck said to the night.

"What are we forgetting?"

Graneck jumped, startled, then turned to face Termark O'Schoitt. "Nothing." Even as he said it, he knew Termark saw through the thin veil of his fear.

"My daughter scares you."

"And why shouldn't she?"

"I have discussed this with the council numerous times. After months of careful consideration, they determined she was not a threat to us. Why can't you accept that?"

Graneck scoffed at him. "They can make that assumption because?"

Termark let out an exasperated sigh. "Anne was inbred. Much like horses, if a family line does not deviate from its own blood, you end up with a high-strung horse, mentally deficient, that will bolt for no reason. An unstable, unpredictable animal."

"Hmph." Graneck scrunched his face and scratched absently at his mustache. "In my mind, Termark, your daughter is also an unstable, unpredictable animal. Her mana is much like Anne's was - anomalous."

"The seeress Amy cast a chart of Tnasha's stars when she was born. She is quite balanced. Her mana is benign and has no definitive element, though water and earth are strong with her." Termark looked up at the sky. "We are not fools, Graneck. We understand the dangers of sorcery, and I have worked hard to instill in my daughter the responsibility that comes with power."

Termark's argument did not sway Graneck. "She is becoming too powerful. That makes her dangerous. What if she is swayed by an opposing faction of sorcerers? In the wrong hands, and with false persuasion, that power could be used against us."

"Perhaps. She is talented in many areas of sorcery, though not quite adept. I do know one thing though…" Termark leaned in, looking straight into the Priest's eyes. "I did not raise a fool for a daughter. She is not easily swayed. Her intelligence surpasses even yours, dear Graneck. She may be young, idealistic, afraid, inexperienced, impatient, arrogant, and even hasty in her choices, but when it comes right down to it, she rights her wrongs and tries to do what is honorable. That is all any of us can do. We all have the capacity to be dangerous to ourselves and others. Maybe the gods and all that is would see our kind die for that very reason. Perhaps this is why we are now faced with these trials. We are living in a dangerous, war-wrought world. A war of sorcerers."

Termark pointed to Shadon who stood alone near a group of soldiers who sat drinking spiced wine. "His kind, humans, they are trapped in the middle of our war. While our lines die, his flourish. The gods and all of nature know what is best, wouldn't you agree? We only continue to fight in hopes we can save ourselves. Survival, however, is nothing more than an instinct."

"Are you certain?" Graneck gave him a steely look.

Termark half-smiled and said, "Verily."

Verily my ass, thought Graneck. His lips parted, but he couldn't find the right words. Termark turned and walked away, leaving the priest agape and contemplating his own place in the universe.

CHAPTER 17

Behind them, they left Cabalia in ruins, its people murdered. So far, the weapon proved a powerful adversary against the humans. The real test, however, would be Arkeereon. Seth wondered what defenses the Arkeeronish sorcerers would use, or if the Imperial Hierarchy of Arkeereon even knew they were about to be invaded. He smiled thoughtfully. "So, what do you think they will do?"

Alax stared ahead with a blank look in his eyes, as if he was going through the motions of life without really realizing he was alive at all. He answered in a quiet, hollow voice. "Try to save themselves."

Seth ignored his brother's gloom and pressed on. "Yes, but how? I wonder. Will they position themselves as archers and hurl blates of mana? Or will they combine the use of steel and mana?"

His brother turned to him with a dull expression. "I don't know what to expect. We should probably expect both."

"You are not enjoying yourself." A hint of disappointment rang in his voice.

Alax groaned. "No. I have a bad feeling. I'm also tired."

The self-appointed Kersian monarch shook his close-cropped blond head of hair in defeat. "You're being irrational, brother. I've had many bad feelings in my life. In my experience, bad feelings are a prelude to victory."

"Or a slaughter." Alax scowled.

Seth looked back at the carted weapon. Upon cursory glance, it looked like an unremarkable catapult. The only distinguishing feature was the black stone that gleamed in the sunlight. The four bay geldings that drew the cart ambled alongside them, a few of them dragging their hooves. He shrugged. "Us, or the Arkeeronish?"

Alax lifted an eyebrow. "It could go either way."

"You're not afraid, are you?"

"You keep asking if I'm afraid, and I keep telling you I am uncertain. So yes, I suppose I am afraid. That comes with uncertainty." He shrugged, then yawned and rubbed his eyes.

"Good." Seth nodded. "Fear makes one more aware on the battle field." With that, he leaned forward in the saddle and put his heels to his horse's ribs, urging the unkempt gray mare into a weary jog.

Looking over his legions, Seth realized they weren't as pristine as he'd hoped. Many of them wore rumpled uniforms and smelled of iron and sweat. Nonetheless it empowered him to ride at the front of his legions. Behind him, his soldiers followed in obedience. They killed at his command, loved at his command, and died at his command. Life was good. The fear and respect they showed him when they cowered or lowered their eyes pleased him. Fear commanded respect. Just as the thought occurred to him, the mare beneath him stumbled and slowed to an amble. One of his commanders rode up beside him.

"Stupid beast." Seth looked over at the soldier. "What's wrong with this horse? She obviously has no stamina."

"Sire, we should stop and rest them more. This mare may be unfit for riding if we continue." The commander looked down, afraid to meet Seth's gaze.

Alax urged his horse into a trot and rode alongside them. A mark of anger crossed his face. "He's right. We need to stop and rest the horses, or they will drop dead outside Arkeereon."

"Afraid we won't be able to retreat?" Seth sneered at his brother and narrowed his eyes. He would have to have a talk with Alax later about questioning him in front of subordinates. "There will be no need to flee."

Alax let out a sigh. "That is *not* what I meant. I am simply considering that we need to take care of our horses. Our soldiers risked their lives to steal them. They are a valuable commodity for us. One we cannot afford to lose."

After a brief moment of consideration, Seth nodded. "Very well put, and your reasoning is sound. Fine." He lifted his voice to his legions. "We will rest here. Set up camp!"

From the corner of his eye, Seth saw Alax breathe a deep sigh of relief. Maybe his brother didn't have any more stamina than the mare.

***

They stopped on a hill, in a clearing surrounded by trees. A stream ran through it. Not only was it a good vantage point to watch the valleys below, but it offered shade and water. Alax looked up at the sky. It was late afternoon. He'd scarcely slept the past few days and he could feel exhaustion settling into his bones.

Seth was a good soldier, but in Alax's opinion, he was not a good leader. He yearned to tell his brother how careless and haphazard he was. Seth always acted without thinking things through, but Alax held his tongue and presented the matter with diplomacy. It angered him that Seth would be so careless with the lives of the horses, especially when he often made mention of Gavgal's carelessness with the beasts. He wondered then how many lives would be lost, both animal and human, because of Seth's impatience and lack of foresight.

Alax's thoughts ground to a halt. Could it be that his powers of persuasion had more impact on Seth than he thought? Those powers just didn't work on Seth the same way they did on humans. He dismounted and loosened the girth of his saddle, giving his bay mare an affectionate pat on the back. Alax was grateful to have a horse at all. More importantly, however, for the first time he realized how grateful he was to be a sorcerer. He could affect change. Perhaps in that, he could save his brother from getting their men, and themselves, killed. For now.

Once the mare had been cooled down, fed and watered, and her hooves had been cleaned, Alax left her to rest. Warily, he approached his brother, who sat on a fallen log along the dirt path. He noticed how Seth rubbed his thumb with his forefinger with nervous impatience. "Relax, brother."

"If we wait too long, survivors of any of the cities of Cabalia could warn the Arkeeronish."

"You said yourself that it was likely they would know we were coming. They have seers, don't they? Perhaps you shouldn't have lain waste to the Cabalian cities just to test the weapon. There was time enough to test it on Arkeereon first."

Seth looked up at him with narrowed eyes. "You are trying to say something?"

Alax measured every word before it fell from his lips. Much like the soldiers, he did not want to risk angering his brother, either. "I am merely saying we should practice patience. If we are too hasty we could inadvertently cause discord for ourselves."

"You aren't turning spiritual on me, are you?"

He shook his head with a smile. "No. I realize my priestly title is only for show."

Seth nodded. "We will wait an hour or two for the horses to rest."

"Ideally we should take five hours. Perhaps even overnight for as hard as we've run them."

"But we gave them breaks."

"Short increments like those only prolong exhaustion. You know this, Seth. You have commanded troops for how many years now? The horses need real rest. So do the men. So do I. I think it may be wise to allow everyone some sleep as well. They will be more alert." He looked at his brother with expectation, wondering what was going through Seth's mind. Did he think Alax was trying to usurp his leadership?

"I am grateful to have you as an adviser, Alax. You keep me balanced." Seth stood.

Alax wasn't sure what to make of his brother's statement. "I'm going to take a few hours of rest for myself."

Seth yawned and quickly brought his hand to his mouth in attempt to hide own exhaustion. "I suppose I should rest as well."

As Alax walked away from his brother, a tight smile tugged at his lips. Even if Seth did not mean what he said, it was true in the implication that he needed Alax. Without him, Seth would have gotten himself killed long ago. No, Seth was no great leader, but what man was? Behind every powerful man there were advisers, and in many cases - those advisers were the ones with the true power.

CHAPTER 18

Aithian and Tnasha sat together with the whole of the Imperial Hierarchy of Arkeereon in the great hall of the holding. There, they waited. The Eagle's Talon sat propped against her lap. Natyis still found himself blinded by the radiance of Tnasha's mana. Natyis had confided in her that his sight vanished in her presence and clouded all situations with which she was involved. Now, they relied on Tnasha's use of the Eagle's Talon and the visions it brought her. With it, she watched the Kersians make their way through the Cabalian port, leaving nothing but ash and cinder in their wake. The powerful weapon had destroyed the city in five blates and Tnasha could still hear the roar of flames and the screams of the dead. The Danarian warships had dropped anchor not long after and sent their legions ashore to follow the Kersians inland.

She braced her hands on her knees and took deep, measured breaths to regain her bearings after the frightful visions. "At least we have my people taking up the rear."

Lucas, Aithian's longtime friend and Tnasha's newly found one, snickered. "Usually that position should be reserved for an ally."

Tnasha smiled, looking into the stone as it glowed a brilliant gray light. "Will you trust me? Did I lead you astray on Zul?"

Lucas thought about the question for a moment. "No."

"You actually had to think about that?" Her voice hinted disappointment.

Aithian grinned, amused.

Tnasha's gaze wandered to Morvack, Seth and Alax's estranged traitor brother, who sat huddled near the back wall with the young sorceress who was now his wife. "Morvack?"

Looking at her with fearful eyes, he said, "You don't know Seth."

"Oh yes, I do. I remember him well," Tnasha said.

Aithian and Lucas nodded in agreement. They remembered Seth, too.

"No." Morvack's voice shook a little, tinged with fear. "You don't know what his mind is capable of contriving. This weapon you told us about should prove how he is. There is something *not right* with him. He is ill-tempered and tyrannical."

Verrine leaned forward. "That sometimes happens to men who are field soldiers. If they spend months and years away from home, fighting wars and living out of a satchel, then they start to lose their mental faculties."

Tnasha nodded. "Our physicians call it battle sickness. But we cannot forget that Seth has Alax. I wouldn't be surprised if Alax is helping guide Seth. Usually, men with battle sickness act rashly, and end up dead or captured…" She stopped mid-sentence.

Something in the midst of the stone atop the Eagle's Talon distracted her. The stone swirled gray again. She peered into it, narrowing her eyes as if it would help her to focus better. It was of no use. The images there were hazy. They moved quickly in and out of her mind's eye in no particular order without making sense. Something wasn't right.

"What is it you see?" Natyis asked. He leaned forward in alarm. The members of the Arkeeronish family lines began fidgeting nervously.

"More fire. Knives. Blood. Screaming. A loud explosion." She felt the blood drain from her face. Jerking away, she tried to pull her mind from its connection with the stone, but it sucked her in, pulling her deeper and deeper into the chaotic vision.

Aithian pulled the staff from her grasp, hiding the stone from her field of vision with his hand.

Momentarily dizzy, Tnasha closed her eyes until her head cleared again. Her breathing slowed gradually until she felt more like herself. She opened her eyes only to find dozens of curious faces turned towards her. "We have to leave. Now. I can't tell if it has already happened, or what will befall us if we stay put."

"We will stand and fight," said the red-haired sorcerer they called Flereous. "This is a battle we can win."

Tnasha turned to him. "It will be a slaughter. The weapon is too powerful."

He drew his sword. "You would have us run and hide? Like cowards?"

"No, I would have us live. I never said we would hide," she shot back.

"And where would we go to *not* hide?" A condescending smirk crossed his lips.

"If we can get out of here..." She paused. "They are near. Very near. If we can circle around and meet with the Danarian troops at the rear, we can surround them or at least get away."

Flereous narrowed his eyes, stood, and stomped to the other side of the room in a huff.

All eyes turned to Natyis. He was their elder, and leader. It was the burden of the dominant male to make such decisions. "I cannot see."

Tnasha grabbed the staff from Aithian and passed it over to Natyis' old hands.

He shook his head. "You do not understand, child. My sight does not work with this staff. My mana is incompatible with its construction. Yours is not."

"But all I can see is chaos. I cannot control the visions, nor sort them into coherence or timelines."

"Will your armies ensure our safety?" Natyis raised an eyebrow expectantly.

She was confident her father would see things her way. She would insist if she had to. "I will make sure of it."

"Then we must leave. There are tunnels past the crypts of the holding that lead to a quarry southwest of here."

Tnasha's hand instinctively went to her waist, where her sword and dagger usually hung. A gripping panic sieged her stomach and she suddenly felt vulnerable. Danger was eminent, and she had nothing to protect herself save her sorcery, which had proven itself unreliable in the past. She sighed. *At least my magick has ultimately saved me, even if it was cast with dumb luck*, she thought. She sat back. "I need a sword."

"Steel won't work against the weapon, remember?" Flereous came back over to where everyone sat and stood behind her.

Strangely, his mana scarcely flickered, staying as smooth and non-aggressive as many of the sorcerers in the keep. It made it hard for her to sense him coming. "It would make me feel safer."

He reached into his mana and pulled a short sword out of it, handing it to her. "Here."

"How…"

Natyis let out a strained chuckle. "He's been able to do that since he was a child. Keep items inside his mana."

She took the sword from him and tried to put it into her own mana. It didn't work.

Flereous laughed.

She gave up and instead felt the weight of the blade in her hand. It felt good, and even though ridiculous, it made her feel safer.

"Are the tunnels secure? Any chance of a cave in?" Eury asked. "We don't want to be buried alive."

Natyis looked over at him with a shrug. "I don't know. They were built for this very reason, yet we have not had need of them for centuries."

Tnasha stood, and the others did the same. "We don't have any more time. Take only what you can carry, bring lanterns, and hurry to the crypt. Put out the torches and hearths behind you. Stay away from the windows."

Lucas gave her a half-salute, prompting Aithian to respond with a nervous laugh. They hurried to gather what they needed. As dusk approached, the holding stood silent with the baited breath of the Arkeeronish sorcerers who gathered down by the crypts of their long-dead ancestors in anticipation of doing what had to be done.

***

Natyis stood near the door leading from the crypts to the tunnels.

"Are we doing the right thing?" Eury looked at the door, which was small compared to the size of a man. The tunnel would be small, tight. They would have to go through it hunched over. The women and children would pass more easily. Regardless, the width of the door suggested the passage did not promise to be wide, either. He shuddered.

"I cannot see that we have a choice. Lucas and Atanchia have secured the gates and doors. Perhaps when we return..." His voice trailed off.

"We are returning..." The hope was clear in Eury' voice. "Aren't we?"

Natyis' look became somber, and a flash of worry crossed his white eyes. "I do not know," he said, quickly shifting his pale gaze away.

Eury lifted his voice in protest. "But this is our ancestral home..."

The elder sorcerer, within whom the blood of the ancient family line Natyis flowed, lifted an old hand to silence his friend. "What the sorceress has seen is a vision I've ignored for far too long, Eury. Before my sight was taken, blinded by her mana, I foresaw this day. I thought it was *what could be*. Now I know it is *what is*."

"What," Eury paused, almost afraid to ask. "What did you see after that?"

A thin smile covered Natyis' lips. "Vindication, rebirth of that mana lost with our ancestors' lives, and survival."

"So, then we will come home?"

He shook his head with a resigned sigh. "No. A new home awaits us. It will not be without its problems, but we shall prevail."

A thought struck Eury then. He narrowed his eyes.

Natyis nodded. "Yes, my friend. I cannot see, and haven't been able to see anything around the sorceress. I could only feel that we needed to bring her here. Admittedly, I speculated that she was a pair bond to Aithian, as that made sense, and still does. But it has now become apparent that there was a larger, more dire reason." He turned then and put the key in the lock. As he turned it, the mechanism clicked open, several tumblers gave way, and the door opened, unbarring their path.

Eury leaned forward with the lantern, looking into the ancient hallway that ran beneath the holding and the Arkeeronish city. It was dark, narrow, filled with dust, and thick with webs. He had nothing to say. What could he say? Natyis' predictions were uncanny and always correct. Even when the old sorcerer was blind.

***

Tnasha and Aithian stood at the back of the room while, one by one, the members of the Imperial Hierarchy of Arkeereon disappeared into the dark depths of the subterranean tunnel. Aithian took her hand into his sweaty palms. She gave him a reassuring smile and tightened her hold on him. No matter what happened, she was not going to let anything happen to them. Even if the Kersian's did find them, she had decided that she would lay down her own life to save theirs if need be. With a deep breath, she stepped into the wretched tunnel. Aithian, being the last sorcerer to enter, swung the door closed behind them.

Chapter 19

Flames and thick, acrid smoke met them at the port at Cabalia. Steadily, the three ships dropped anchor in the port and unloaded the men and horses. Enough men had been left behind to guard the ships, though judging by the state of Cabalia, it would have done little good if the port was attacked again.

They'd been riding for some time now and Shadon couldn't shake the bad feeling in his gut. It was the same feeling that overcame him on the warship, but it was stronger now. The stench of death hung heavy in the air. The Kersians could not help but destroy everything in their wake. It was the way they were and would always be. Nothing would ever change that. So far, the Danarians had traveled through several cities fallen and burnt to the ground. Shadon fought the urge to cover his nose with the gray scarf he wore around his neck. The smoldering scents of scorched flesh and burnt wood could sour anyone's stomach.

"I wish there were a way to kill them off once and for all." Termark's voice was tight and strained.

Shadon glanced up, knowing Termark was talking about the Kersians. "We shouldn't come in directly behind them."

Termark turned to him with a clenched jaw. He said nothing.

Shadon smiled sheepishly. "Sorry. I shouldn't tell a warlord how to do his job."

Ignoring Shadon's apology, Termark turned his horse toward the soldiers, rose up in his stirrups, and called out, "We will come around the southwest side of the city and try to curtail them that way."

The sour feeling lifted from Shadon's stomach. Perhaps all he needed was some reassurance. He looked around. Arkeereon was a flat land. The few trees, fields of crops, and piles of rubble that had once been buildings, did little to make it more interesting. In the summer it was too warm, and in the winter, too cold. With a small military and even less leadership, it surprised him Arkeereon had managed to remain a country all its own. "Probably because no one would want this heap," he muttered under his breath.

Termark chuckled. "You're absolutely right. No kingdom in the West Ocean Mainlands has any use for this place. It's a wasteland that reeks of decay. Though I suspect it has more to do with the rumors that it is the land of the dead."

Shadon lifted a wary eyebrow. "Land of the dead? You're serious?"

Termark gave a nod. "It is said that long ago this land was fertile and even had hills."

"Mountains?"

"No." Termark scrunched his nose. "No, they were hills. Allegedly, a large group of sorcerers once ruled over all Arkeereon. The Natyis family sect. When the Kersians took the only daughter of the elder Natyis and sacrificed her to the nameless god, he became angry and split the world, leveling all of Arkeereon, and rendering the northern lands barren in the process. He cursed the land so that any Kersian who walked on it would fall to an uncertain fate. The sorcerers who live here are the remaining progeny of that family line. That is why no human kingdom has come here to claim the land their own."

"And if the sorcerers left?" Shadon found himself disturbed by the tale. Not because it was unbelievable, but because it wasn't. He had seen what Tnasha could do, and if the ancient Natyis, as rumored, could manipulate all of the elements with his sorcery... Shadon shuddered.

"If they left, undoubtedly this ancestral land would eventually be taken over by human colonies. New kingdoms and governments would emerge."

"And more of the sorcerer race would die out," Shadon finished.

Termark nodded.

"So maybe it wouldn't be a bad thing, necessarily, if Tnasha was to help them continue their family lines. Or any other Danarian sorceress for that matter. I mean, after all, the larger the pool of the opposite sex, the more bloodlines would flourish to keep all the family lines going, right?" He glanced sideways to check Lord Termark's reaction, fearing his opinion might be considered reckless among the sorcerers.

Termark said nothing, which only added to Shadon's fears. But he had to know. "Wouldn't it?"

"Extend the family lines? Yes," Termark finally said.

For whatever reason, Shadon sensed that maybe Lord Termark was in denial and did not want to consider this. "So why is it such a big deal if Tnasha fell in love with an Arkeeronish sorcerer? I sensed something between them." He stopped short when he felt Termark's eyes on him.

"We have a very selective process by which we pair bond sorcerers. A male and female may choose their pair bond from within a select group."

"Selected by the parents?" Shadon knew very little of sorcerer relationships except that two mated sorcerers generally begot a child with more mana than its parents.

"By the temples and the elders." Termark lifted his hand then, signaling to the legions behind them to move south. A silent relay of hand gestures moved hundreds of Danarian soldiers south, and Termark rode ahead.

Shadon found himself alone with Graneck. Shadon's nostrils flared. As usual, the priest had made sure to stay just at the edge of hearing and had been listening to their conversation all along.

"A sorceress like Tnasha would probably not be allowed to have children," Graneck said, attempting to continue the conversation.

"And why is that?" Shadon did not bother to hide the distaste in his voice.

"She is dangerous." Graneck had said this at least a million times since they began this journey, but this was the first time he sounded unsure of himself.

"I might consider her haphazard. Untrained as of yet, but certainly not dangerous," Shadon said.

"You were simply lucky she did not kill you during your travels with her."

"Perhaps. But she wouldn't have done it on purpose." Shadon turned to him. "Why are you so afraid of her?"

Graneck glared at him and rode ahead without answering.

"You're a wretched bastard," Shadon said beneath his breath. He knew Graneck heard him, but his patience was spent. Feeling a certain satisfaction in angering the priest, Shadon followed with a smug smile.

It was just outside the city, in the dead of night, that Shadon felt her. Tnasha had something he could never place his finger on, but now he knew what it was. Presence. He wondered then if that was why Graneck feared her. After all, it was not common for mere humans to know when they were in a sorcerer's presence. The others must have felt it too, for Graneck lifted his eyes, ears, and nose and sniffed at the wind like an animal, as if trying to find her. Termark's eyes went in the same direction Shadon's heart pulled him. Shadon cursed under his breath. The buildings of this southern far end of the city hid her. Where was she, and how was it he could feel her?

In the distance, to the North, Shadon saw the outline of Arkeereon. From the city walls smoke lifted skyward, and they could hear the wind howling. What served as the military of Arkeereon would surely be dispatched in little time.

The Kersians had not reached the holding yet. It stood a huge black mass of stone and mortar against the bright, moon-filled sky. The sorcerers of Danaria's armies whirled about suddenly, drawing their swords as if they had heard something. A sickening chill swept over Shadon.

Without warning, the sky suddenly lit up with a blast of fiery light that struck the holding, cutting through the first fortification wall. The horse beneath Shadon shifted nervously. Not because of the sound, as Shadon expected, but because the ground beneath them moved each time the fire took to the air, and struck the quiet black holding of the Arkeeronish Sorcerers.

Shadon's senses gave in to his fear, and his brain moved with methodical accuracy. "A holding that size - tunnels. There have to be escape tunnels." The soldiers and sorcerers turned to him. "But to where?" He looked around in the darkness, absentmindedly scratching his forehead. "Somewhere with cover." He turned to Termark. "Hills."

"South," Termark agreed.

Graneck looked on with disapproval. "Hills?"

"An ancient mountain range, long sunken into the earth. They do have quarries," Termark moved forward, leading his armies onward without question. "We have to get to them before the Kersians do."

Shadon smiled in triumph. They were no longer there to wage war. Survival was all that mattered.

With each blate of fiery mana breaking through the holding in cascades of thunderous booms, the sound of rock exploding broke the still night air. The Danarian legions hurried onward once again, driven by instinct.

***

They spotted them along the bank of a steep incline. Single file, from the black depths of the earth, a line of various colored lights emerged into the darkness of the night. Termark's eyes scanned the darkness for the violet hue of Tnasha's mana. Just when he thought his daughter wouldn't be among them, he saw her followed by a single bright blue-gray light. The last in line. He breathed an audible sigh of relief. One by one, each light, each mana, dimmed and faded black. They were hiding their mana as they emerged into the open.

"Stay here and keep a lookout for the Kersians. I will go to meet them alone." Termark rode forward, allowing his horse to carefully pick its way down the steep embankment.

Once he reached the bottom, he urged his mare into a gallop. Tnasha stepped out of line, allowed her mana to glow softly, and rushed forward to greet him. "It's my father," she called back over her shoulder.

Termark stopped several paces in front of her. "Are you all right?"

"I'm fine, but we need to get out of here. It's only a matter of time before they come this way. We have women and children here who won't stand a long walk."

"All of our men are mounted. On foot, we would have no way to outrun them." He peered back up the embankment to the unseen legions waiting there in the darkness.

By moonlight, he could make out the grim expression on her face. "We cannot fight their weapon. We do not have enough adept sorcerers here."

"We cannot outrun them, we cannot fight them…" Termark lifted his brow in thought.

Someone stepped up behind Tnasha in the darkness.

Termark lifted his chin. "Who is this?"

Tnasha looked back over her shoulder, then back at her father. "This is my friend, Aithian."

He lifted an eyebrow and gave the young man a nod. Then he turned to Tnasha. "We need to get far away from here. There is no time for discussion. Come." He held out his hand, offering her to share his horse."

"What about the women and children?"

Termark looked over the multitude of shadow-figures standing in the darkness. "How many are there?"

"At least fifteen," she said.

He knew she was guessing. He turned and motioned for his soldiers to ride down. "The men will have to walk unless we can come across some horses."

Tnasha took his hand, and he lifted her up onto the horse behind him. "What makes you think we'll come across any horses?" She sounded doubtful.

"Because the Kersians destroyed everything in their path before getting here. I suspect some of the horses must have gotten away."

She put her arms around his waist and leaned into him. "Father, they've just lost everything. Including their horses," she murmured. "Could you please be nice?"

"I know," he whispered back, hoping she knew that he understood her compassion for the Arkeeronish. He couldn't help but feel it, too. He wasn't a monster devoid of feeling.

It took a little time, but finally, with the women and children riding with the Danarian soldiers, and the Arkeeronish men walking quickly alongside them, they headed west, back toward what remained of Cabalia. There, their ships waited. It was clear to Termark then that the only place the war would be won was on Danarian soil, by their terms, standing together. Having the Arkeeronish sorcerers only strengthened that position. What Danaria had that the Kersians did not, was greater numbers and enough sorcery to make the Kersian's deadly weapon seem like a single crossbow.

CHAPTER 20

Seth seemed to enjoy the destruction almost too much. He led the way, hacking and slicing through human meat and bone. Alax kept himself out of harm's way by staying behind the fight with his sword drawn, just in case the onrush of human resistance reached him. He had no need to fight because the soldiers did it for him. He was no warrior, but rather a diplomat. At this moment, Seth had no need for advisers or diplomats. Alax watched as his brother leapt atop the carted weapon, pouring mana from himself into it. Then he directed it in fiery blates, giant balls of fire, that crashed into the Arkeeronish holding with startling precision. The sorcerers were probably sleeping. Unless they had foreseen it and hidden. But if they hadn't, then they would be buried beneath the crumbling walls of their holding.

Finally, when the threat of opposition had passed, Alax rode forward alongside the stationary cart. "Seth, you should rest. You will imbalance yourself."

Seth turned to him, his eyes a fiery red. "Do you propose to destroy the rest of it?"

Alax's eyes traveled over the skeletal remains of the structure. "There is no need to reduce it to rubble completely. You have likely killed them all already. They probably didn't even see it coming."

"We will wait until morning then. Search for survivors, and bodies. I want a body count." Seth smirked.

Alax yawned. He was tired and in no mood for Seth's want for a significant death toll. "Fine. In the meantime, it looks as though your men have effectively destroyed the entire city. Should we search for more survivors to torture and kill?"

Seth waved his hand. "Let the men do what they will."

"Very well." Looking over the destruction, he shook his head and left Seth standing amid the remains of the destroyed city.

Finding and rounding up the horses proved to be more of a chore than Alax anticipated. The chaos had scattered them all around the city. As he found them one by one, he brought them to the roped off corral he had made between several trees at the city's edge. The light of the moon was enough to light his path. Some of the horses were undoubtedly not theirs, but it didn't matter. The horses that were too exhausted would be left behind. They would need fresh mounts.

Physical work stilled his wandering thoughts, but they eventually broke through to the forefront of his mind. He hurried from the corral to find his brother.

He arrived to find Seth overseeing his human army as they entered the fallen holding. So far, they had found nothing.

"They weren't in there!" Alax's voice pierced the night air. Seth and his men stopped in their tracks.

"How do you know?"

"They had to have a seeress. A group of sorcerers that large has to have at least one." Alax's breath came quickly, in shallow gasps. His lips trembled with anger. They had been made fools of! "If they were taken by surprise they would have fought back no matter what the odds. But the holding remained quiet the entire time, because they were not there."

Seth narrowed his dark eyes. "Go on."

He shrugged. "They escaped. They could have left days ago."

"Where would they go? To the desert south of here? They could be seaside by now."

Heat rose up Alax's neck into his cheeks. Seth's lack of common sense had grown tiresome. "Well, they did work with the

Danarians to save their precious staff. They are obviously allies. Where do you think they went?"

Seth's response emerged from his lips a low, malicious growl. "Danaria. We will crush them."

Once again, for what seemed like the fiftieth time that day, Alax shook his head. "We can crush them later. I suggest that instead of wasting our time searching for something we will not find, we should rest and move out in the morning. Being on the ship will allow plenty of time for you to devise a battle plan. In the meantime, you and your men need all of your strength. We will gather the survivors and offer them food and shelter for their service as soldiers to replenish our troops. I'll be sure to use my *gift* to encourage cooperation."

Looking down on him from his vantage point atop the cart, Seth's lips contorted into a frown. "My brother is correct," he said to the soldiers listening in on the conversation. He jumped down from the cart.

Alax took a step back when he saw his brother's expression.

"You could not have told me this earlier? Alone?"

He swallowed hard. "It just occurred to me that this was possible."

"My men probably think me a fool." Seth's eyes bore into him, accusing and cold.

"They wouldn't dare," Alax said reassuringly. "You could kill any one of them with a single blate. They know that and would not oppose you. Besides, you have the greatest weapon of mass destruction ever created. Not even I would oppose you, Seth. Insurrection is the least of your worries."

Seth's frown slowly turned into a half-smile. He was convinced. "Yes. You're right."

Alax smiled back at him. Not because he believed what he had just said, but because he knew he had just saved himself from his brother's unpredictable temper.

***

Seth needed silence. He was convinced that what he sought was some place beyond the noise of sorcery and the hushed whispers of his men. The only man who remained a mystery was Alax. At times, it seemed his brother continually tried to override his authority, and that made Seth furious. The anger was becoming increasingly more difficult to control. As he thought about it, he realized that it had been a long time, beyond any recent memory, since he was without anger.

He could remember every single one of his men who had died serving the Kersian empire. Their pain, their last cries. He even remembered, in clear detail, how each of them looked in death. Thinking back, it dawned on him that he stopped caring about their deaths. He had to. It was the only way he could erase the pain and guilt he once felt for sending so many people, his brothers in arms, to their deaths.

It was Gavgal's fault. Seth frowned at the thought. Gavgal got exactly what he deserved, and Seth felt no guilt at having killed his brother. In all honesty, he felt completely guiltless. A sharp chuckle emerged from his throat and tumbled out of his mouth, surprising him. He sat down on the ground, looking at the dry dirt. Running his hands over it, he let the texture of the sand press into his flesh. Lifting his hands, palms up, he studied them. "These hands," he whispered. "I can do whatever I choose to do with them."

At that point, he heaved himself from the ground with a shove and dusted himself off. Until now, he had not considered what it was that *he* really wanted. What did he want in a world he ran? A society of sorcerers at the upper echelon with men as his servants, yes. But his thoughts of the dead sorceress flooded his mind more often now. She had been tricky. Strong, stubborn. The ultimate conquest. If there had been one sorceress like that in Danaria, there were more. His new world was all about having his every need and want met. It meant that he would never have to kill again. Never have to feel the pain or anger ever again.

He smiled, deciding then and there that he would try to take one of Danaria's sorceresses as his own, but if she was too stubborn, and resisted too strongly like the one he'd killed, she would have to die. This was going to be tricky, for certainly the females would not be forced from Danaria when the battle started. It was possible they would even be on the front lines with swords drawn, ready to fight to the death and watch their loved ones die around them. In that, both he and the warrior females would have something in common. He wondered then if that would be enough.

Seth shook his head at his own foolishness. No, maybe he needed a submissive woman. There was no way a sorceress of any power or stubbornness would willingly give herself to the man who had killed her kinsman. "Too bad, it was certainly a nice fantasy while it lasted," he told himself.

One thing was for sure, for a moment, however brief, Seth questioned his own motivation, which, unbeknownst to him, is exactly what Alax had told him to do.

***

"Where have you been?" Alax asked from the darkness of the tent they shared. He had not seen Seth for hours.

"Sitting quietly with my own thoughts."

"Oh." Alax closed his eyes as a wave of relief washed over him. Now that he knew where Seth was, he wouldn't have to worry that his brother had continued on his rampage of destruction and death.

"I understand it now," Seth said.

His eyes opened slowly, and he looked over at his brother's shadowed form. "What?"

"When you asked me if my plan was wise. You wanted me to explore my own motivations. I have."

He knew his brother's short, terse sentences where his way of masking any emotion. "And what did you discover?"

"That my new world will be quite peaceful so long and no one steps out of line. Together, we will create a world free from war."

Alax stifled a snort and said nothing. He didn't know what to say.

"I briefly considered trying to keep the warrior women," Seth said with raised eyebrows. "But I realized that was nothing more than a fantasy. They would likely cause too much opposition." Seth looked at his brother expectantly.

"What?" Alax sat up then. "Warrior women?"

"Like the sorceress we killed. They likely have more of them. She couldn't have been the only one."

Alax felt his eyes go wide.

"What?"

"Well," Alax shrugged. The mention of the dead sorceress did surprise him. She seemed to be a subject Seth was fixated on in an unhealthy way. Perhaps the sorceress had gotten into Seth's head, or worse - was haunting him from the grave, if such things happened. "I guess I never expected you to think about women much."

Seth chuckled. "Usually I don't have time for that. I think about women plenty. Now perhaps we should sleep?"

"Yes." Alax pulled a thin woven blanket around him and settled back onto the hard, dry ground and closed his eyes. Weary, he listened to the crickets and the far-off howl of a wolf. His mind drifted to the varying possibilities of the outcome of the coming battle. His stomach growled. The last thought that went through his mind as he drifted off to sleep was the hope for a large, palatable meal when he awoke.

CHAPTER 21

The high priest Gorain stood before the altar, bathed in the bright, white light of his own mana, and that of the air elemental. Before him, upon the stone slab altar, sat a polished ball of smoky crystal. Gazing into the crystal's depth, he saw them: armies of sorcerers defending Danaria from a weapon so deadly that the city stood reduced to rubble. The image changed. Gorain watched as his people, the Angorans, fled for their lives, trying to find places within the Onyx Mountains to hide themselves. But one by one, the weapon hunted them down, spurred on by the unwavering determination of a madman. He gasped and pulled himself from the vision.

A deep unsettling fear washed over Gorain. First, the Kersians had sent a battalion of humans to attempt to steal their women, and now this. While the Angorans had thwarted the former plan and had killed the humans Seth had sent for the task, this was different. Now the Kersians had a magical weapon that *could* hurt them. Gorain had never known fear. Ever since he was a child, he felt safe in the mountains, knowing that he could hide from travelers and watch them pass without them even suspecting his presence. He knew enough magick that he could easily thwart the humans. No, he had never known fear. Not true fear. Now, it tightened its grip on him, pulling him against his will into a dark recess inside himself. Fear was a place he had never explored.

Gorain looked up at the high ceiling of the cave, nestled high in the Onyx Mountains. The cave served as the Angorans' *Temple of The Eagle*, a place where all Angorans believed the Spirit of Air, of knowledge and reason, was present. The soft flicker of several dozen torches bounced off the uneven rock walls and the soft dirt floor. It was a place all the tribes visited at least once a year to perform their rites to the air element. It was here that boys became men and received the tribal art tattooed into their skin in magical inks at their coming-of-age.

The four chieftains of the tribes of Angora stood patiently behind him, waiting. Upon their bare chests, the scars of the tribal rituals, symbols intricate in their mystical patterns of geometric shapes and vivid colors, stood out in clarity against their darker skin and were illuminated by each of their individual colors of mana. Gorain turned to them with a swish of his gray robes. "The war has begun just as we feared."

"We should take our tribes deeper into the mountains," said the first chieftain. His blond hair seemed to match the deep yellow hue of his mana.

The priest, Gorain, shook his graying head of long, disheveled hair. "No. We would run forever. This time we cannot sit idly by and do nothing, Jagon. We must make our stand and fight alongside our own kind. The survival of our race is at stake."

The oldest of the chieftains, Almarg, stepped forward. He put his thick, calloused hand to his long white beard and scratched at it thoughtfully. "We have always remained neutral to the world's affairs. Is there any other way?"

"No. We cannot stand by and do nothing this time. You all know as well as I do that if we are to survive long enough so that our grandchildren may inherit this world, we must stand alongside the Danarians and the Arkeeronish, and defeat the darkness of the Kersians once and for all."

Jagon laughed in arrogance. Gorain lifted an eyebrow. Jagon's father had died the previous year, leaving him the youngest chieftain of the Angorans. "Why do you laugh?" Gorain asked.

"The Kersians are but several sorcerers. The Danarians and Arkeeronish number close to a hundred or more. Certainly, they can defeat the Kersians without our help?" Jagon shook his head, widening his eyes in expectation at the other chieftains.

"The Kersians have a weapon," Gorain explained. "one that would cause the mass destruction of Danaria and all who would defend her."

"So, what are you suggesting, Gorain? That we go to Danaria only to die? How does that save us?" The young man's expression turned sour. He set his angular jaw, and his deep gray eyes turned black. He turned to the other chieftains. "What say all of you?"

Almarg turned from Jagon and met Gorain's gaze. "We stand and fight."

Gorain looked expectantly at the two, middle-aged chieftains who had said nothing. "Will you and your warriors fight alongside us, or will you, too, choose to hide yourselves in the mountain caves and valleys?"

One of them, Calang, of the third Angoran tribe, shook his brown head of hair. "And wait for them to hunt us down? No. My tribe will fight."

The final chieftain, Drago, of the second tribe, nodded in concurrence. "My warriors will not run."

With a final shake of his head, Jagon turned from them and strode from the great Angoran *Temple of the Eagle*. Gorain let out a deep sigh. "He is a foolish young man, not ready to lead his tribe."

"Perhaps it is for the best. A man who does not believe a battle can be won, brings upon himself, and his warriors, the certain fate of defeat," Almarg said.

Gorain nodded. "Then we must prepare. We shall perform a rite to the spirits of our warrior ancestors for our victory."

Together, the four Angoran sorcerers made their way from the temple to the clearing outside where all but one of the four tribes of Angora sat waiting for them.

One of the priests went to the south-most point of the clearing and raised his hands above him, intoning the vibrational invocation of the fire spirits, while the other priest stood in the east of the clearing and intoned a different vibrational invocation of the spirits of air. Gorain stood in the middle of the clearing and raised his arms on high.

"Come forth the warrior spirits of Kunuck. Bring our warriors strength and bring us victory!"

The priests then began the methodical task of anointing each warrior with the oil of air, to give each one clear sight and a clear head during what was sure to come.

With their rites complete, and their people surrounding them, Gorain assembled the chieftains before the crowd.

They spoke amongst themselves for a moment, but Gorain did not hear what they were saying.

Finally, he turned to the waiting eyes and ears of the Angorans. "There is a grave situation upon us. Even now, the Kersians are making their way toward Danaria with the intent to destroy our city dwelling kinsman, the Danarians. But they will not stop there, my brothers and sisters. The oracle has shown me that if our Danarian brothers fail, the Kersians will leave no stone unturned, no cave unexplored, until we exist no more. These chieftains who stand before you have chosen to stand alongside the Danarians. To fight with them. Jagon has decided that his tribe will stand alone, here, in the mountains, and face whatever fate befalls us. We will leave the women and children behind with enough warriors to defend them should the need arise. Those warriors who volunteer to stay behind with the women and children will take them into the mountains, perhaps place them with Jagon's tribe. We shall gather our remaining warriors and make haste into Danaria."

Each tribe numbered between fifty and one hundred, and amongst them all, not a murmur surfaced from the crowd.

"If there is anyone who objects, object now," Gorain said. Silence.

With a nod, Gorain turned to the assembled chieftains. "The people have spoken. We move out to Danaria in the morning."

CHAPTER 22

Boarding the ships and making their new guests comfortable had been easy enough, but Termark realized it had taken valuable time. Nonetheless, the Danarians had already weighed anchor and turned their ships back toward their homeland in hopes to be ahead of the Kersian ships by a day or more. Termark had gone below deck to check in on their passengers. He looked over the weary travelers and noticed Tnasha had fallen asleep with her head nestled comfortably on Aithian's broad shoulder.

As he watched her, the warlord felt Shadon come up behind him, silent and catlike. It always amazed Termark how stealthy Shadon was in his movements. He could never feel Shadon's presence until he was within arm's distance. Were it any other person, Termark would have been nervous, but of all the humans he knew, even those he called friend, he trusted Shadon most. He did not turn to face Shadon. "Look at her. You were right. For a human, your insight is uncanny."

"Not so much as Seeress Amy." He chuckled lightly, causing several of the sleeping sorcerers to stir.

"Had we listened to Graneck…"

"But you didn't," Shadon paused. Termark knew he was looking around for any sign of Graneck. "Graneck is a fool driven by his own insecurity and fear."

Termark turned to the tall, lithe spy, looking him in the eye. "Fear? Graneck?"

"He fears Tnasha, doesn't he? He can't control her and therefore he fears her. In that way, humans and sorcerers are very much alike."

The warlord nodded. "We want to destroy the things we fear."

"His fear is driven by his inability to understand or control her ability."

A man's voice came at them from the left. "And her ability grows even now."

Both Termark and Shadon turned to the source of the voice, realizing Lord Natyis, now awake, or perhaps awake for some time, now stood next to them. He wore a cowl-hooded robe to block out any light. Termark looked at the cloaked figure and shuddered, hoping his discomfort was not visible. He had not felt the sorcerer wake, or move towards him, either — and that fact disconcerted him. "If her abilities keep growing, what then?"

"She will adapt," said Natyis. The Arkeeronish elder tipped his head toward her. "She is, perhaps, one of the most stubborn females I've run across in all my years. Her power will grow to fit her environment, and she will adapt to it."

"But Graneck won't," Shadon said, twisting around again for any sign of Graneck.

Natyis looked down on the still figures of Tnasha and Aithian. Around them, their mana moved in harmonious synchronicity. Tnasha's hand clutched the Eagle's Talon that lay across her lap. "A pair bond. I knew it the minute I saw them together. So, you can understand my reasoning in doing what I did."

Termark bit his lip. The elder had given him the perfect opportunity to discover why he had abducted her. But Termark could not bring himself to ask the questions. He could not find the words.

The blackness beneath Natyis' hood dissipated and from behind the folds of thick, black fabric, his white, glowing eyes became visible: all seeing and all knowing. "My hierarchy is dying out, Lord Termark. There are three generations of sorcerers here, and yet only four of them are children. Our men outnumber our women. One pair bond, perhaps more in the future, means more children, and the bloodlines continue."

"You should have asked. We could have avoided all of this." Termark heard the anger in his own voice and sucked in a deep breath to calm himself.

"Would you have agreed?" Natyis shook his head. "Had you agreed, we may not have survived the Kersian attack. If there is one lesson I have learned all these years it is this, everything happens for a reason. Amid the chaos of the universe, there is order and balance. We may not know the effects of our actions until well after we do what we do, but on reflection, everything happens as it should."

"You mean prophecy?" Termark narrowed his eyes.

Natyis shook his head again. "I would not call it that. Prophecy only has the power to suggest a general fate. No. I believe the universe has already scribed, in great detail, the pages of each living thing's life path."

Shadon snorted. "That's nonsense. That would mean you have to believe in fate. That you have no control over your own life, and that your decisions are all preordained by something you can't see. Much like the Kersian god."

"Religion is something our families abandoned long ago. Nothing comes of it except pain and death." Natyis shifted uncomfortably and his eyes settled on the stairs leading to the deck. "The Kersian sorcerer Seth has abandoned his God, too. But he has nothing to believe in except his own need for power. He is lost and angry and unsure of himself. If you do not mind, I would like to go up to the deck for some fresh air."

Termark and Shadon stepped aside wordlessly, allowing Natyis past them. They followed. Surely Graneck would be waiting to corner Natyis in conversation. The High Priest took every opportunity to put his nose where it didn't belong. Termark had long ago disregarded it as an inherent flaw in Graneck's nature, but he did not want that flaw to cause more discord. They couldn't risk it. Even now, undoubtedly the Kersians were only a day behind them, following with the weapon. Right now, Termark only had enough patience to fight one battle at a time.

***

Sweat trickled beneath Tnasha's clothing, into the crevices and curves of her body. Too warm, she shifted around in discomfort and stood. She rubbed the sleep from her eyes. Around her, the room sat silent with only a single lit lantern to cast its light on one corner. The shadowy figures, bathed in brilliant colors of mana, moved restlessly on the floor. She hurried over them to the steps leading above. The thick, dark air suffocated her. Finally rising from the darkness below, she emerged onto the ship deck, finding relief in the cool, humid air outside. Shielding her eyes from the bright gray light of a cloud-covered sky, she made her way to several wooden boxes where she could sit and acclimate herself.

Graneck appeared beside her, at the very edge of her field of vision. From the corner of her eye, she saw him hold a metal cup, steaming with hot liquid, out to her. She looked up, up, and up, shielding her eyes again.

"Take it."

"Is it poisoned?" She lifted a wary eyebrow and reached for the cup.

Graneck's voice rang out into the wind, which carried it away from her ears. "It is tea. Nothing more."

She took it from him, not sure she wanted to welcome the liquid's warmth against the palms of her already warm hands. Putting the cup to her lips, she sipped at the light brown liquid, letting it slide over her lips and tongue, and make its way down her throat. She nodded. "Good. Though I could have done with something cold. Wine perhaps." Graneck's offering of tea still baffled her. Maybe he was just humoring her in hopes she would swoon over the gesture and offer up secrets in exchange. It was a little late for that, but who knew what was going through the priest's fevered mind. "So why is it you're bringing me tea? Aren't I the enemy? A dangerous sorceress who must be destroyed?" A forced laugh escaped her lips.

"I was asked to bring it to you."

"And you agreed because?"

He frowned and looked down at her with uncertainty. "Because I was not doing anything else."

"Why, by Natyis," she stopped and smiled again. So much for the phrase *by Natyis*. Now that she knew Lord Natyis it seemed silly. "Why are you here at all?"

"I came along so we could find you." His answer was plain, simple, and curt.

She rolled her eyes and sighed, knowing Graneck must have had an ulterior motive. "You wanted to make sure Danaria's most volatile weapon didn't fall into the hands of a possible enemy?"

Graneck did not answer.

"I don't understand you." She looked beyond him to both her father and Lord Natyis, who both walked toward her and the high priest.

"Well, perhaps you should stop trying." Graneck took a step back, put on a forced, welcoming smile, nodded at her, and walked away.

She looked down and studied the tea.

"Was Graneck bothering you?"

Tnasha looked up at the sound of her father's voice. "He was merely making sure I," she paused, unsure and tired, and not wanting to discuss it. "Nothing. I don't know." She lifted the cup. "He brought me tea."

Natyis' gaze shifted to Priest Graneck, who leaned against the railing of the ship, watching them from the distance. "Does he not like you?"

"He fears I am dangerous due to my... anomaly." Tnasha motioned toward her mana, aware of the blatant sarcasm in her statement.

Natyis turned from Graneck to Tnasha. He lifted a dark eyebrow, accentuating his abnormal, white eyes with the pupils black slits in the center. "What you call anomalous, we call elemental."

"There is no violet elemental." She looked up at him, puzzled.

"To my people, sorcery is an element in and of itself. What is your god-name?" Natyis smiled down at her, genuinely interested in her answer.

She shrugged. "What is a god-name?"

"Each Arkeeronish sorcerer bears his or her god-name as a first name. It seems your families have not kept with this tradition."

She sensed the disappointment in his voice but realized then what he was talking about. "Oh. My God-Name is Delepitore'. But it is my third given name, before my fourth. The Sorcerer High Priest Kalath gave it to me when I was an infant."

Natyis nodded. "Of sorcery. How apt. You, Tnasha, carry the mana of all sorcery within you. You are the force that binds the elements in a constant stream of flowing energy."

"But Natyis - the element, I mean - Natyis is all that is." She tried to remember back to the days when her parents sent her to the temple to train with the priestesses, who had eventually given up on her due to her stubborn nature and unwillingness to participate.

Natyis shook his head. "Natyis is the fifth element. That from which all things come. If we were to look at the image of a pentacle as a representation of the elements, your elemental mana would be that which encircles the others. My mana may be the source, but yours is a strong part of the balance." He rubbed his hands together. The air grew cooler.

For the first time, it made sense, and the fact that it made sense frightened her. It was no wonder she was able to do things she could do, though she still hadn't figured out how to carry a sword in her mana. Tnasha shuddered, realizing how visible her discomfort was. Natyis said nothing, simply watching her.

Tnasha's mind raced. Clearly, the knowledge of sorcery, and the knowledge of sorcerers themselves, was strong with the Arkeeronish as it was with the Danarians. She had ample opportunities to learn, but instead chose to ignore those who offered to help her in hopes no one would pay too much attention. Now, she realized that being a sorceress was something she simply was, and nothing would change it. It made sense how the priests and priestesses had paid her so much attention, and why other sorcerers would stare at her. They were in awe of the brilliant flowing stream of elemental violet mana that emanated from her. Had she taken the time to learn, she would have known this. Regardless how much she did not want to be the focus of others' attention, she was bound to her mana eternally. With that bond, came responsibility so great that she suddenly knew it was the *responsibility* she had spent her life fearing, not the sorcery itself.

This realization made her stomach queasy. She looked up at the Arkeeronish elder, wide-eyed. "That's it. That's why it's so easy when it isn't forced."

He smiled. "Of course, it is." Tnasha could see his insight into her in his eyes. For all his years, Natyis' certainty comforted her. It was the first time since Kalath that she acknowledged an elder's wisdom and actually believed in it.

She returned the smile, saying nothing, and sipped at the tea, longing to be home, within the castle holding, in her own chambers near the warmth of a bright hearth. Aithian would be there with her, cradling her in his strong arms. There she would be safe from the brutal world outside the high walls of the castle, and beyond Danaria's strong fortifications.

***

For the first time in Tnasha's presence, Natyis could see far and clear. He could not have prepared himself for what he saw when he looked at her. A cold chill overcame him, followed by an overwhelming sense of fear and need. Longing, warmth, insecurity, happiness, sorrow, and anger all leapt out at him. The emotions were so intense that he feared he would react to them. Never before had he delved so deeply into anyone whose emotions ran with such turbulence. The young sorceress that sat before him was, perhaps, the most conflicted spirit his mana had ever touched. She deeply loved Aithian, but her sense of duty and responsibility kept her from loving him like she wished.

Natyis then sent his senses searching for Termark amid the men on deck. Somehow, the weight of all the world's problems had been set upon on Tnasha's shoulders. Natyis could not allow the young woman to carry the burden alone. She struggled with the responsibility in silent fear, and without complaint. But it was time for all sorcerers to share in their fate. One sorceress alone could not save their bloodlines, nor the world. But all of them, together, could. He knew that Termark understood this, but like his daughter, he needed nudging to realize his insights were correct.

CHAPTER 23

Tnasha wished that everyone on board the ship was feeling well and rested. She knew that, even together, there was no way they had enough energy that they could open a portal and transport the entire ship and its cargo, the sorcerers, straight to the port at Danaria. Everyone looked worn and haggard. What they needed was a good night's sleep and a solid meal to fill their bellies.

Shadon approached her and sat next to her on the wooden crates. "I see you're getting yourself into trouble again." He gave her a wry smile and shoved a dark lock of his hair out of his face. "What happened?"

She looked around to see if anyone was listening to them and once she was sure that their conversation was somewhat private she said, "The sorcerers needed me. Our bloodlines are dying. The seer, Natyis, knew that I would be needed to help them get away. If the Kersians catch up to us, were in a lot of trouble. We don't have magical weapons like they do, and the sorcerers are all exhausted. It doesn't bode well for using magick against magick."

"There's something different about you," Shadon said. "I think maybe you've grown a bit battle weary."

She forced a laugh. Maybe everything that happened in the past few months had forever jaded her or made her more cautious. There was a time not too long ago when she would've thrown caution to the wind and done something reckless. "I suppose. All I know is we're at a crossroads, and if we don't figure out something soon, then Danaria will fall and the sorcerer bloodlines will be wiped out. If Seth gets his way, he would have all the humans enslaved and worshiping him as a god."

"Men who see themselves as gods are nothing more than tyrants. Tyrants are arrogant and prone to making mistakes. Fatal mistakes," came the heavily accented voice from behind them. Shadon and Tnasha turned to see Natyis standing there.

Tnasha ran her hand through her auburn hair and stopped to massage her scalp at the back of her head. More than anything, she wanted a warm bath. She drew in a deep breath of brackish air and exhaled a cool mist. "Then what's the plan? How do we get Seth to make such rash mistakes that he jeopardizes his own chances of success?"

Both men must've thought it a rhetorical question because neither offered an answer.

"No, I'm serious," she said. "We need a plan and I hate feeling unprepared."

Natyis patted her arm. "No. You hate being without a clear mission. There is time to come up with a plan and I'm sure that's what all of the people on this ship are attempting to do."

Tnasha's heart palpitated in her chest, and she felt short of breath, so she took another deep inhale and closed her eyes. Natyis was right. She did hate being without a mission. "Time without a purpose is a waste."

"Don't worry," Natyis assured her. "I see more clearly now, and what I see gives me hope."

With that, the Arkeeronish elder moved off toward the railing of the deck, and Tnasha turned her attention to Shadon. "Seers and their archaic responses. How can he say something like that and just walk away?"

Shadon chuckled. "If you knew everything that was going to happen, that would take the fun out of it."

She smacked his arm. "There's nothing *fun* about this."

"Well, maybe you should come up with a plan, too. To make yourself feel better, I mean." Shadon lifted a thin hand and motioned toward the other men on the deck. "After all, Tnasha, you're not helpless or naive like so many of these men seem to think. Don't you get tired of feeling like a pawn in their game? You're a powerful sorceress."

"I wish people would quit saying that." She snorted and rolled her eyes.

Shadon raised his brow, "Why? It's true. Maybe you should start acting like it."

His words were like a slap across the face. "Fine," she said. She bit her lip and looked around. "Where's the water, or the wine? I can go either way."

Shadon pointed to a barrel sitting underneath the eve of the ship's cabin. Standing, she walked away from him and got herself a drink. She lingered at the water barrel, staring into its depths as if it might hide the answer. If it was, it was doubtful she'd be able to conjure it at will. Nothing came to her, and she turned to see that Aithian and her father had joined Natyis and Shadon near the railing of the ship. The wind picked up, and she heard whipping fabric in the breeze. Looking up, she saw the sails unfurled. She had been so preoccupied that she hadn't noticed them before.

"We have air, wind sorcerers," she whispered aloud to herself. That was it. That was the answer. If she could convince Lucifer and Lucifuge to work together, perhaps with her help, they could use the wind to move their ship faster and reach the Danarian mainland more quickly, leaving the Kersians far behind them. It could give them a few days advantage. The trick would be to make sure the wind didn't help the Kersians along, too. She started toward them, her feet feeling like lead but her mind racing with hope.

She interrupted the group, not caring what their conversation was about. The four men looked up at her approach, their faces showing anticipation in response to the mask of urgency covering hers.

"Wind," she said plainly. "We need wind and a lot of it. Where are Lucifer and Lucifuge?"

Natyis smiled. "Now you're thinking like a sorceress. I'll gather them."

Shadon regarded Tnasha uneasily, trying not to cringe. "Are you sure about this?"

If anyone had been witness to her magick failing more than it worked, it was Shadon. He and Kolgern, of course. But Kolgern wasn't here, and it was only Shadon who bore the memories of all of her failed sorcery. "This time, if I fail, at least we can blame Lucifer and Lucifuge, too. Together maybe we won't mess it up."

Aithian gave her a supportive smile, but he didn't say anything. Her father did the same.

Great, she thought. *More silence.* She glanced upwards. Heavy, gray clouds overhead threatened rain. *Why could dire situations never produce better weather?* She wondered.

Then she looked at Aithian and narrowed her eyes. "Is it possible you could clear all of this rain and nasty weather out of the way?"

"I could," he said. "But weather like this makes for better wind-working."

She shook her head. "I'm not a mariner, but I do know that if the weather stays like this, we risk crashing into the rocks on the shores of Danaria, which would do us little good. We need to be able to see where we're going, and in this murk, we'll be lucky to see twenty-five miles ahead of us. If the weather gets worse - even less." She gave all three a smug look, knowing she was right.

She half-wished they would argue or say something—anything—that meant the weight of this plan didn't rest on her shoulders alone. She kicked herself inwardly. It was easy to get wrapped up in one's own emotions so deeply that one felt like they were drowning. One. She smiled at her own stupidity. She wasn't talking about *one*; she was talking about herself.

Natyis returned with Lucifer and Lucifuge in tow, both bleary-eyed and trying to shield their gazes from the light. Even though the sun hadn't even broken through the clouds, the gray skies were still much brighter than the cargo holds below where it was black as pitch. Both men looked exhausted, but their mana appeared strong and moving.

Natyis gestured to the trio. "Now, between the three of you, what you need to do is draw the wind to blow upon our sails and our sails alone, in the direction of the Danarian mainland. I know this will be taxing and you will be exhausted, but the quicker we do this and arrive safely, the faster we'll all be able to get some sleep and food." Natyis gave Tnasha a nod, urging them to try the magick.

The three sorcerers grouped themselves together, huddling tightly behind the sails to be certain that they were pushing the wind in the proper direction.

"Should we hold hands or something," Lucifer asked, first looking at his brother, then at Tnasha.

Tnasha shrugged, taking up one of their hands in each of hers. "Now focus," she said. "Close your eyes and draw the power of the wind through you, forcing it into the sails, pushing us further and further toward home." She stopped herself and quickly corrected her instruction. "My home, not yours."

Lucifuge chuckled but didn't say anything. The brothers, as if by symbiotic connection, each lifted their free hands, pushing the wind through them, using Tnasha as the conduit between them to draw more energy and throw more force behind their sorcery. The wind vibrated through them and through her, blowing their hair about and shaking their bones. Every inch of her being vibrated with a cumulative energy that thrummed through her head. She gripped their hands tighter.

The ship began to move forward faster and faster, cutting smoothly through the water. They were able to keep up the momentum for some time but after a while, fatigue began to line the brothers' faces. Lucifer and Lucifuge had to stop and so she stopped too. Their arms still wrapped around each other, they stumbled back to the stacked crates filled with who knew what and fell against them. It felt good to sit, to relax, and to not feel the vibration of the wind running through her.

No one was sure just how many miles their wind magick had brought them. Tnasha fell asleep right there on the deck, and when she woke up the sky was clear but black, filled with tiny pinpoints of light. Stars, so many of them, flooded the night sky. At least now the sailors could navigate and make sure they were on the right course. With any luck, they'd be able to find their way to port without too much hassle, and with more luck, the Kersians had been left far behind.

Aithian sat next to her dozing off despite himself but waking every few seconds as if to make sure she was there. She took his hand in hers and leaned into him, feeling him relax. "Now on to the next part of the plan," she said.

"What's the next part?" he asked, daring to put his arm around her and pull her closer to him. A brave move for a man who could be confronted by a woman's father at any moment.

"I have no idea," she said with resignation. And she really didn't know. Maybe that was the trick. Figuring out the plan, each step, as they went, but not being able to think any further than that step.

"I think the next part of the plan should be making it to dry ground safely, and then making our way inland to central Danaria as quickly as possible. Bring together the troops and anyone who will fight, and let the military commanders work out the details on everything except the sorcery." Aithian looked down at her and pressed his forehead to hers as if urging her not to worry.

She was good at worrying, though, and no amount of wishing that she wouldn't fret over every detail would make it any less so. "Military commanders can't fight sorcery with sorcery. We need an army of sorcerers. The Angorans will have to gather up their tribes, collect their horses, and commit to fighting. That means soliciting help from Graneck. I saw him somewhere on the ship, but he's made himself scarce since. He can be a right beast that one."

Aithian chuckled. "If he has the resources, I don't see why they shouldn't be utilized."

She looked up at him with a crooked smile. "You just referred to sorcerers as resources."

A flush of crimson rose into his neck. "You're right. I did. By resources, I meant soldiers. I guess it's easier to think of soldiers as resources when you know at least one of them is going to die. Makes it less painful when bad things happen."

"I suppose that's why they call them troops. It dehumanizes them." She leaned back against his shoulder and thought about this. Was that why the sorcerers' race was dying? They were dehumanized by being called sorcerers? After all, sorcerers were just humans who were born with the mage blood. With mana. While they may have been rare, they were still human. *Rare humans*, she thought.

It was no wonder there was such rivalry within most cultures across the West Ocean Mainlands. She leaned further into his chest and lay there listening to the beating of his heart while looking up at the sky. She didn't want to talk anymore, to think anymore, or to do anymore. Not tonight. She just wanted sleep, and maybe find some food.

It was Lucifer who brought back food for everyone: dried meat, cheese, and ale. There was little else. The last crusts of bread had dried long ago and were not fit for human, sorcerer, or mouse. As they ate, Lucifer passed on the galley cook's promise of hot gruel for morning breakfast. They took their time relishing the meager meal. After they'd eaten, she and Aithian retreated back down below to the sleeping quarters. Together, they found a quiet corner and huddled against one another for warmth with only Aithian's cloak for a blanket.

Traveling was a dirty business and even though Tnasha could handle quite a bit, she hated feeling dirty and smelling like livestock. Dirty bodies jostled up against each other in the cramped quarters, reeking of sweat, flatulence, and rotting meat. Their journey couldn't be over soon enough, which is why they were all rather relieved that afternoon when they finally heard the cry of, "Land Ho!" from the crow's nest on the main mast.

They made it, surmising the wind magick had brought them several hundred miles in such a short time. With any fortune, that left the Kersians at least one or two days behind them. Their other advantage, of course, was that they knew their way to Central Danaria and could use the well-groomed main roads to travel. It would be faster that way. The Kersians would have to lay low and find their way through thick forests, rolling plains, and finally through the mountainous regions to the well-fortified borders of Central Danaria. That could, realistically, put the Kersians another day or two behind.

Tnasha's spirits lifted as the boats' passengers surged out onto solid ground, many of them whooping with joy. The ocean journey had not sat well with some of the women and a few of the men, who'd gotten seasick, several of them for the entire journey. But once everyone was back on dry ground, their spirits lifted and all of them appeared to regain a brighter outlook and more energy. The port at the city was able to provide enough food, horses, and wagons for the journey into Central Danaria. While they didn't have time to stop and bathe or change their clothing, they did have time to stop and eat.

Never before had fresh bread, vegetable stew, and roasted meat tasted so good.

Tnasha marveled at all the things she'd taken for granted growing up. Safety, clean clothes, water whenever she wanted it. Food whenever she wanted it. And good food - not dried meat and stale cheese. Never crusts of bread, or scraps. Indeed, she had lived a very privileged life and she found herself thankful for the experiences that had shown her that.

Instead of riding, she decided to stay in the wagon with the rest of the women to get more rest. A sorceress who was exhausted was worthless, and she was going to need all of the energy she could muster, especially if she wanted her magick to work the first time. *Perhaps that was one of the secrets of good magick*, she thought. *A well-rested sorcerer.*

This revelation caused her to open her eyes and look around at the dozing women in the cart her. That was it. The sorcerers would be strong if they worked together and drew energy and strength from one another. Alone, they would tire more easily. They could be stronger than any magical weapon Seth could wield. The humans who weren't magically inclined could take on Seth's human armies, while the sorcerers themselves would deal with Seth and Alax. The Angorans, coupled with the Arkeeronish sorcerers, and the few Danarian sorcerers outnumbered Seth and Alax by at least one hundred and twenty-five. This was the next part of the plan. They would have to set aside their differences and cooperate, allowing whoever led the campaign to take control and direct the others. That, she surmised, was where difficulties would arise. Graneck would likely be the biggest obstacle since he would want to be in charge. Then again, perhaps one of the Arkeeronish sorcerers would challenge for the position. If Tnasha were to take the lead, who besides Graneck would challenge her?

She paused, wondering if she should really be in charge of something this important. Perhaps it would be prudent to stand down and allow one of the others, a more experienced sorcerer, to take command. Those old feelings of being inadequate, of being a weak female, reared their ugly heads and manifested as a knot in her stomach. Deep inside her, a fire burned - a deep determination to show everyone that she could do anything a man could. Even if that meant leading a sorcerer army against Seth and Alax. That's when she decided that she would have to, in some way, be the one to lead the sorcerers, and if anyone opposed her, she would deal with it when it happened.

The journey would have felt like forever had she not slept a large part of it. When she saw the castle, her heart leapt with joy. She didn't recall ever being so happy to see home. Well, maybe she'd been this happy at least twice in the last few months. No matter, she was home, and she knew home and was comfortable here. She knew that her magick would do well in familiar surroundings. She wouldn't have to worry about a strange environment because she knew what the threats were. Comfort in magick could make all the difference in the world, she decided. It was a theory that still needed to be tested, of course. Perhaps it was also a good argument for her to take charge of the mission.

The Arkeeronish sorcerers shifted uncomfortably, looking out of place. Their clothes were tattered and their faces tired, too tired to be afraid. They'd just lost everything. What little personal items they did have, they carried with them in satchels. It wasn't much. Their castle holdings were no more, crumbled by Seth's magical weapon. They were people without a land, and Tnasha sincerely hoped that her people would warmly receive them. She could not have been more pleased to see the scores of men and women who came down to greet the carts and carry what needed to be carried, all while leading the tired travelers to their quarters.

The Danarians took every opportunity to make sure their guests felt welcome and comfortable. Even the priestesses from the temples brought extra food and clothing, and they offered to help carry water for baths. The kitchens bustled with frenzied cooks hurrying to make a feast of a meal for their guests' homecoming. Knowing that the Arkeeronish were looked after, Tnasha could finally look after herself.

It wasn't until after she'd bathed, slept, eaten, and felt human again that she was summoned to the Great Hall to meet with heads of state and military leaders. Tnasha decided to wear dark leggings and a rather masculine jerkin, along with a sidearm - her short sword. The Eagle's Talon sat firmly in the grip of her left hand. She figured the men would take her more seriously if she was armed and looked somewhat sorceress-like. Natyis sat on the far end of the table with Eury to his left and Aithian to his right. Graneck sat at the head of the table. A second high priest was present. It was Ragok, and Angoran who she found an unfathomable pain. She arrived during an argument about how to fortify the city against the oncoming invasion force.

"We need to go through and weed them out," one general said. "Last time we stayed inside the city and waited. We cannot waste time like that again."

Then the room went silent. It was as if her mere presence made them uncomfortable. Priestess Caitlan was the only other woman.

"Is that a magical weapon?" The high priest, Ragok, asked, his voice laden with disdain for the weapon's unassuming appearance.

She looked at the staff, then at him and said, "No. It's a scrying device."

Tnasha had no intention of letting them know that the staff had more powers than just allowing its bearer to see the future. She was confident now that it was the staff that helped her to open the portal that helped her escape Zul only months ago. She still had no idea what all it could do. Regardless, the staff had chosen her as its bearer, and as far she was concerned, it was hers. She didn't care if the Arkeeronish claimed it was theirs. It always seemed to find its way back to her possession. No one had stood in her way when she took it and carried it with her through the tunnels underneath the Arkeeronish holding, to the shores where the ship waited, and finally to Central Danaria itself. Natyis probably knew that the staff was hers, and that's why neither he nor his brethren contested her ownership of it.

"Come, Tnasha, sit," her father said.

She took the chair offered her and laid the staff across her lap. The men began arguing again.

"We should set magickal traps around the city," Ragok said.

"That would take too long and exhaust our sorcerers. They would have no energy to fight," Graneck countered. "Danaria is a large city, not some small village."

Natyis held up a hand to stop them. "Perhaps we should ask the sorceress what she thinks about magical protections."

The priests, commanders, council members, and generals looked at each other, then at Tnasha.

"While I certainly respect that Tnasha has earned the respect of a soldier, I don't see what she can offer in a battle plan that we cannot." The commander who spoke looked offended.

The head general, Kale, stood and tipped his head thoughtfully and said, "Yes, but she is a sorceress and she may know things about sorcery that we do not."

The high priests both snorted.

Ragok shook his head. "She is a child. Natyis here, he is a sorcerer too. And yet no one seems to be seeking his opinion or counsel."

Ragok's issue with Tnasha wasn't the same as Graneck's. Graneck thought she was dangerous. Ragok thought she was an impetuous child.

"Because the prophecy centers around Tnasha and no one else in this room," said Caitlan with spite.

Natyis nodded. "I agree with the priestess. While this will affect all of us, the prophecies all center around the sorceress. Tnasha has a plan."

All eyes moved to Tnasha and she felt small and uncomfortable in their gazes. She was right to feel that way, of course, because they *were* judging her. She could almost feel them asking themselves if they could leave the fate of their entire city and the sorcerers' race in the hands of a young woman. It was written in their expressions. She wondered then why prophecies never centered around people who were emotionally stable and wise. People like Kalath and Natyis. Their advanced age made them learned and rife with experience. She drew in a deep breath. *This is all a manifestation of your own insecurity, Tnasha,* she thought.

"I, for one, believe we *should* have the most powerful sorceress in all the land at the helm. Do you have a plan?" The general asked. At least Kale was willing to hear her out.

With a nod she swallowed the lump in her throat. "We need the humans to take on the human threat, and we need the sorcerers to deal with the sorcerers. This means that the human generals and commanders will deal with their forces and us sorcerers will dispatch Seth and Alax. I propose that *I* lead the sorcerers into battle."

Tnasha glanced at her father, afraid of what she might read in his expression, but his face was blank. Either he was going to great lengths to hide his emotions from her, or perhaps he really did think she was competent.

No one said anything, so she fumbled onward. "When I worked with Lucifer and Lucifuge with the wind magick on the ship, and we held hands and used one another to ground each other and draw energy through all three of us – we were strong. We had real power and focus and the magick didn't go bad, or create mishaps," she tried to explain. "I think that's what we need from the sorcerers who will defend this city. A willingness to work together and support one another. We are stronger together than alone. Seth and Alax can fight each of us alone. But together, a hundred or more against two, even with their magickal weapons – we are a powerful force. One that won't be defeated."

General Kale nodded, and a slow smile spread over his lips. "I think that's a good plan. In which case, gentlemen, my commanders and I will work out our plans for the city's defense. We will coordinate with the sorcerers and help them separate the sorcerers Seth and Alax from their armies, so we can fight each independently."

Tnasha liked how the General slipped a very good suggestion in at the end, and she gave him a knowing smile. He winked at her, then turned, and with his commanders standing to follow, left the room.

CHAPTER 24

"**W**here did they go?" Seth's eyes blazed fury, and the ship helmsmen stood helpless against his mask of anger.

Alax shook his head. "Obviously they used sorcery to get away. That much is clear. It doesn't matter how they did it, only that they did, which means we now have to hunt them down."

Seth rolled his eyes. "It also means they now have time to prepare a defense."

A deep sigh emerged from Alax, and he rubbed the sweat from his forehead. His clothing clung to his body in the humidity, and every part of his body ached from the sea voyage. He knew it would be over soon, but that offered little comfort. Deep down he knew they were likely marching to their deaths, and in some strange way, he was at peace with that. Instead of speaking his mind, he looked his brother straight in the eye and smiled. "The Northern side of Central Danaria is our best hope. It's not easily defended and offers more cover."

Seth grumbled. Alax knew his brother's armies had been defeated there before.

"You know as well as I do that it offers the most coverage to hide our armies." Alax knew his brother didn't want to hear it, but there was no point in feeding him false hope.

"They'll be expecting that," Seth growled.

"Perhaps they will, but what choice do we have? Do we run back to Zul and hide? Wait for them to come after us? Or do we take action now? We have the weapon this time." Alax motioned toward the thing, now secured with lashings to the deck of the ship.

This seemed to reinvigorate Seth's optimism, and he nodded in agreement. "You're right, Alax. I knew there was a reason you were my favorite brother. We anchor in shallow water North of Morasta. We'll use a raft for the weapon and the boats for the men to get to shore. The horses can be led to swim behind the boats to dry land. Once there, we make our way to the northern entrance of Danaria," he instructed. The nearby captain and commanders nodded.

Alax forced a smile at his brother. "The weapon will make easy work of their destruction this time."

Seth nodded again, his gaze already far away, perhaps imagining their victory among the bloodshed sure to come.

Then Alax turned toward the starboard railing and drew in a deep breath. Magical weapon or not, he knew they'd never see Zul again, and he felt nothing but relief.

CHAPTER 25

Tnasha arrived at the library, face flushed and winded. "Sorry. I was out at the stable looking in on the horses."

Termark smiled and cradled the warm cup of tea in his hands. His daughter had always liked horses. "I wanted to talk to you - specifically about Graneck and the Angorans."

Tnasha sat down in the matching high-back chair next to him and gave him a confident nod. She was no longer the child he'd raised, but a strong-willed, responsible woman. "I know all about the Angorans. Don't forget that they sent assassins to kill me. Notice how it didn't work out for them. Of course, I have no delusions that I'm their best friend, and I have no doubts they may make an attempt on my life again."

Termark wasn't surprised by her response. She had grown a great deal. Were it a mere half year ago, she might have panicked at this news, but today she took it in stride. "And Graneck? I've heard many rumors about him."

"So have I," she said. "I heard he colluded with the Kersians."

"But we have no proof," Termark said. With a sigh, he leaned forward. "I just want you to be careful. Priests have a nasty habit of using poison. My own sources have suggested Graneck and the Angorans aren't the only ones who consider you dangerous."

"Then I suppose I should probably keep several antidotes in my possession if I plan on living." She smirked. "I suspect he doesn't have a lot of support, especially among the Council. And certainly not among the military."

Termark knew that when Tnasha smirked it meant that she was nervous. He was certain his daughter would never show weakness, defiant to the end. "Unless he's convinced them that you're dangerous. Play into a man's fears and you can control him. It's one of the oldest methods of manipulation, used by leaders to control their people and to draw support for their cause."

"I think Graneck secretly wants to lead. He does appear to like telling people what to do." Her smirk softened into a smile, and for a moment Termark remembered the little girl he used to take fishing.

He'd been hard on her, but it was for her own good. She knew she was different and that she would be a target because of it. Being hard had helped her become the strong woman she was. He was certain of that. He just hoped he hadn't made her too demanding, but then he had also seen the warmth and affection on her face when she looked at Aithian. Perhaps it wouldn't be so bad having an Arkeeronish son-in-law.

"Father?" she asked, regaining his attention. "Is there a plan to deal with Graneck and the Angorans?"

"I hadn't really come up with anything specific. Not yet. What I'd like to do is find a way to get them to reveal themselves for the enemies that they are. Publicly. It's easier to deal with an enemy you can see. Especially in the court of public opinion. I sincerely doubt the bulk of Danaria's residents would want to see their crown sorceress strung up by a bitter priest and a group of tribal ruffians." Termark stood. "Do you want some of this tea?"

She shook her head. "No, I was hoping to get a good night's sleep before tomorrow. I suspect I'll have to wake up at dawn and get together with the sorcerers. We will need the time to organize. I figure the Kersians are only a few days behind us. I want to go to the temple library and go through their books on magic. See if I can find any spells or formulas to create shields to thwart a magical weapon." She paused, looking thoughtful for a moment. "Perhaps a spell to steal magical weapons without them even knowing…"

Her voice trailed off. Finally, his daughter was thinking like a sorceress. Termark smiled wistfully. Kalath had told Termark she would, but that it was going to take time. In that moment, he missed the old man. It was a shame he was dead. He'd been like a grandfather to Tnasha.

Despite his momentary melancholy, a rush of excitement ran through Termark. "Perhaps you've found the solution. Maybe you should go to the library tonight."

"If I go tonight, there's the possibility I will run into Graneck. This late at night there would be no one else around, which would be dangerous. If Graneck attacked me now, I would attack him back, solidifying the fears of those who oppose me, gaining me more enemies than friends. Priests stand with their own most of the time."

"What about Caitlan?" Termark suggested. "She rarely stands with her temple brothers."

Tnasha laughed. "Caitlan fans the flames wherever she goes. She's stubborn. Why do you think I like her?"

Termark laughed.

She stood to and started toward the door. "I certainly hope we don't have to call anyone out publicly as my enemy."

"Nor do I," Termark said. "I will think on this more and see if there is a way we can reveal them without causing excessive discord. Perhaps we can employ Shadon to watch them closely and keep us informed of anything. Plots and the like." He stood, strode over to her, patted her on the shoulder, and together they left the castle library, Tnasha going one way and Termark going the other.

CHAPTER 26

In the tower room of his quarters, overlooking the temple courtyard to the fountains below, Graneck paced the length of the room. The soft orange glow of the candles and hearth only reinforced his gloom. He didn't like this. He didn't like it one bit. The sorceress - she had too many supporters. It was a problem, and the girl had grown more brazen in the last few months. He'd hoped that the failures would wear her down, break her, and turn her into a mewling mess as it might have for most women. But she wasn't most women. The girl was downright stubborn and rejected authority. She went out of her way to rebel against social conventions. It made her possession of such powerful mana even more dangerous. Even in the temple, she had friends. Priestess Caitlan for one – another woman who rejected authority. Graneck didn't like mouthy women, or women who tried to tell men what to do. They disrupted the balance of things. That's what Tnasha did, she disrupted the balance. The balance of nature, the balance of patriarchy, and the balance of power in Danaria.

His heart quickened with anger. Matters were spinning beyond his control and it sickened him. He was the one they should have been listening to. In matters of spirituality and sorcery – it was supposed to be the priests who gave the orders and dictated the rules. Sorcery was a spiritual art, one that dealt with gods and powers far beyond the limited understanding of the average man.

Graneck drew in a breath and looked out the temple window into the black, star-filled sky. He had no plans to take over the council or lead Danaria anywhere, but he would be content to lead the temple. Priests had their own governance. Overeducated and full of themselves, many would have liked the title of Temple Overseer or Grand High Priest for themselves. And if they had to cut a throat to get it? He shook his head. Perhaps he was deluding himself. The Council was likely the same way, and the military leadership. Military hierarchical structure made it difficult to take over without starting a coup, and one would need a great deal of backing from powerful soldiers in order for a coup to take hold. High offices were often bestowed upon men for their allegiance to someone in the Council who had pull. The temple didn't work like that.

A light knock on his chamber door took his attention away from his thoughts. "Enter," he said.

It was Priestess Caitlan. *Interfering where she isn't wanted*, he thought bitterly. "To what do I owe this pleasure, Priestess Caitlan?"

"I spoke with the seer after the Council meeting this evening," she started.

"Get to the point." He didn't care if his response seemed aggressive or angry. The last thing he needed was another meddling woman who had no business sticking her nose in the affairs of men.

"In our conversation, he suggested that perhaps you did not want to see..." She paused as if thinking of the right words so as not to offend him. "...Us succeed against the Kersians. You would rather see Seth and Alax turn Danaria to rubble, before acknowledging that Tnasha could lead the sorcerers to victory against the magical weapon."

"It's no secret that I think the girl is a fool and has no business leading anyone. She's dangerous. We both know this, and yet you persist and try to think the best of people." With pursed lips, his eyes narrowed, and he raised an eyebrow.

"And you, Graneck, along with the Angorans, have little faith in the sorceress. You think the worst of people. You place such high expectations on them that they could never meet them - even if they tried. Yet what have you done to offer your leadership or guidance aside from criticism? You do nothing more than point out what the leaders and soldiers have done wrong without offering solutions, or suggestions for improvement. You are nothing but a critic, Graneck. A critic who does not want to see others succeed offers nothing to the cause. He's as worthless as any helpless bystander." She smiled sweetly despite her cutting words. Worse yet, she stayed firmly put in the doorway, as if demanding a response.

Graneck stared back at her. Her words cut him like a sharp blade rending flesh from solid bone.

"Well, say something," she finally said.

"I do not need to justify my every action or thought to you, my dear priestess."

"Yes, that's exactly what I thought," Caitlan said with a frown. "You are weak, Graneck. Stick with the gods and do not meddle in the affairs of the military or the High Council."

This time, she did turn to leave.

"Do not tire me with your insolence, woman. It is you who should keep your nose out of affairs that you do not understand," he spat at her back.

She turned to him. "At least my interference benefits all of Danaria and this temple, Graneck. Your interference only serves to benefit your ego."

Then she left, and she didn't look back. Graneck slammed the door after her. After he rid Danaria of sorcerers, include those pesky Arkeeronish, and more importantly, Tnasha, he would have to do something about Priestess Caitlan.

CHAPTER 27

The Angorans had assembled a Council of their own. Now Gorain looked out over the other tribal chieftains and called the meeting to order. "They're letting the sorceress lead us in the fight against Seth and Alax and the magical weapon."

The tribal leader Justan stood and held up a hand to quiet the murmuring group. "If you recall, two of our own were hired to assassinate the sorceress." He pointed to two of the men standing next to him. "They do not think she is dangerous because they've had the opportunity to fight alongside her, which is the reason she's not already dead. They saw proof of her bravery. I trust their assessment that she would do a fine job. I think we should support her."

Gorain slowly nodded. If Justan had been influenced by the stories circulated among the tribes regarding the wondrous staves, it was doubtful any of them would be against her.

One of the assassins leaned forward to Justan's ear and whispered something into it. Justan nodded and then turned his attention back to the tribal Council. "We have been sent word that the sorceress may have an idea that could stop this war before it even starts. I think we need to give that a chance, but also consider the original plan if it fails. It's always good to have options."

Gorain nodded again. "What say all of you?"

More murmurs and exchanges of whispers moved around the tribal Council like the buzzing of bees. Finally, one by one each tribal leader placed his disk of decision on the stone table. The wooden disks were painted red on one side and green on the other. Once he noted each chieftain's disk had been placed there, Gorain again nodded in acknowledgment. All of the disks were green. "Very well. The sorceress has the support of every Angoran on the continent of Danaria."

CHAPTER 28

Despite the need to sleep, Tnasha lay awake staring at the high ceiling of her chambers. Aithian didn't stir one bit when she sat up and threw her legs over the side of the bed. She couldn't stop thinking about the staff and the powers it had that she had yet to explore. Would she find the answer in the stone atop the Eagle's Talon, or in the temple library? She needed to sift through books of spells to find the right one. Using magic to steal the weapon from Seth and Alax seemed an easier task than actually fighting the weapon directly. At least if they removed the weapons from the equation, then the battle came down to nothing but sorcery against sorcery, and their two sorcerers against one hundred Danarians left little room for failure in apprehending Seth and Alax. Honestly, she wasn't sure what Danaria's high Council would do with them once they were caught. It was rare Danaria put prisoners to death unless their crimes were heinous, but it was impossible to keep sorcerers in a jail cell. Eventually, they would find their way out. If Alax and Seth were left to their own devices, this situation would repeat itself over and over again until it was resolved.

Tnasha slid her feet onto the cold hardwood floor and walked across the room to take her robe off the hook on the wall. Wrapping it around her shoulders, she went back to sit on the bed, debating whether or not she should put on slippers. It wasn't like she could go to the temple library tonight and risk being caught, especially by Graneck.

"What now?" she whispered to herself.

"Sleep is always a good idea," Aithian said from behind her, causing her to jump.

She placed her hand over her racing heart and turned to him. "Unholy gods, you scared me."

He rubbed the sleep from his eyes and sat up, yawning. "I can't sleep with all the noise you're making. You should come back to bed and try to get some rest. You're no good to anyone exhausted."

"I know." With a sigh, she scooted back into the bed and sat up next to him against the pillow and headboard. "I'm feeling overwhelmed. Like maybe..."

"I know," he said. "Were I in your position, I may feel the same way. Just know that I stand with you, and I'm here for anything you need. You can delegate tasks to me, I don't mind."

She thought about this for a few moments then narrowed her eyes. "Would you be willing to meet with the other sorcerers in the morning for me? I need to learn more about the Eagle's Talon and the power it holds. See what I can do with it. I also want to see if I can find a spell that can help us steal the weapon from them. If we can get the weapon away from them, we can destroy it. Then we can apprehend Seth and Alax."

"Yes, of course I'll stand in for you," he said.

Tnasha hesitated. The words felt heavy on her lips, but Aithian had to hear it. She had to say it aloud, as much as it sickened her. "We're going to have to kill Seth and Alax no matter what. If we let them go and just take their weapon, they'll be back with more. They won't stop."

"What about Morvack?"

"Morvack was the only smart one of the four," she said of the sorcerer brothers. "Besides, he's loyal to his bride and her countrymen now."

"What if the Danarians or Angorans don't believe that?" Aithian looked at her with a raised eyebrow.

She hadn't considered that. They had been so hurried to get out of Arkeereon that she hadn't considered Morvack was among the Arkeeronish sorcerers and currently slept somewhere inside the castle.

"His appearance has changed so much that I doubt anyone would recognize him, would they?"

"I think everyone's too busy worrying about Seth and Alax to be concerned with him for now. We'll worry about Morvack when it becomes necessary. But once this threat has passed, he and his wife should build a life for themselves somewhere where no one will know who he is." Aithian took her hand in his. "There are some people who deserve a second chance. I think Morvack may be one of them."

"Okay, focus," she said, more for herself than Aithian. "If I can take the magical weapon from them, and we coordinate, the rest of the sorcerers can encircle the encampment. The sorcerers will destroy Seth and Alax, and Danaria's *Sirus Horde* can deal with humans. When you meet with the sorcerers in the morning you will tell them this, and then you all can start working on a plan to deal with Seth and Alax. Though we still need our backup plan if we can't get the weapon away from them."

"I can handle that." He looked over to where the Eagle's Talon was propped against the wall. Its polished stone gleamed eerily in the moon-lit room. "Well, we know you can use that thing to *see* and to open portals. That means someone would have to go through a portal and retrieve the weapon, which is entirely too dangerous for you to do alone. I won't allow it."

Her eyebrow shot up. By the tone of his voice, she knew that this was their first relationship ultimatum. He wasn't going to allow her to put herself in danger any more than absolutely necessary. "Fine. What if I can open the portal, and then use another spell to pull the weapon through it? No one need go through the portal at all."

"That's a much better idea." His body relaxed, and he leaned into her. "I'm pleased to hear you aren't planning on putting yourself in harm's way."

"You do realize I'm a warrior, right? And I can use a sword?" She wanted to say more, but the words came out in a yawn. She snuggled down against him. "You're lucky I'm so tired."

"Indeed, I am," he laughed, wrapping his arms around her. Within moments, they were both asleep.

***

Tnasha inhaled deeply as she entered the library. It smelled heavily of rich leather, paper, and ink. She remembered Kalath telling her long ago that some of these books had been written with bone, in inks made of lamp-black and dyes. The shelves lined with books covered the sounds of her footfalls, absorbing them. She headed straight back to the librarian's counter. One had to check in to be able to read the rare books, and those about magick were kept under lock and key. There was no one behind the desk, so she looked around, wandering through the tall aisles of shelving, each one filled with books. Sometimes Tnasha had thought it would be good to be a librarian, to spend one's day reading. Of course, she knew that's not what librarians did. Sometimes they read, yes, but most of the time they cataloged and shelved books or got them down for scholars. They organized books, so they could be easily found.

She found the frail old priest bent over the cart of books that he dragged down the aisles, taking books from the cart and replacing them on the shelves.

"Excuse me," she interrupted.

The thin, bald man turned to her, revealing dark brown eyes and a pointed nose. His thick brows furrowed when he saw her. "What can I help you with?"

"I'm Tnasha fen Schoitt from the castle. I am here to look to find some spell books." She straightened, pleased with herself for being so direct.

"I see. Priestess Caitlan said that you might show up here someday seeking information. Come, I have a small table and chair in the back you can use." He left his cart and led her to the desk, behind it, and into a small corridor. A door stood ajar to the left of it, and she saw what amounted to a small bedroom. Temple Librarians took their jobs seriously and slept near their books.

He noticed her looking, and he closed the door, instead ushering her toward a door to her right. This one was locked. He pulled a bundle of keys from his belt, clanked through them until he found the right one, then shoved it into the lock. With a grinding of metal, the lock turned, and he twisted the knob, opening the door inward. "In here."

The priest lit a lantern and set it on the table, then lit and took up another to search the piles of books in the room for the grimoire he was looking for. After some shuffling about, he brought two heavy volumes to her and set them on the table in front of her. "There you are. You can start with these. When you're done, knock on the door, and I'll bring you more."

He started toward the door.

"Knock on the door?"

"I'm locking you in. I won't have anything from my rare collection leave this room." Then he left, locking the door firmly behind him.

It was really no matter. Tnasha just wanted to look through books, and with any luck, she'd find what she needed in these two and that would be that. She'd been through all the books on magick in the castle, including those Kalath had left her upon his death. Much of what was in those books was either too basic, or so far advanced she wouldn't have known what to do with it. No, what she needed was an advanced spellbook that was simple enough that a not-quite-neophyte sorceress could figure it out.

Opening the first book, she marveled at how precise the lettering was. Whoever copied this one had taken his time. It was easy to read, and after a short time, she determined that there was nothing useful within its pages. Setting this book aside, she took the second and began flipping through it. This one was riddled with spelling errors, but she could still figure out most of it. It, too, produced no results.

Getting up, she stretched, then went to the door and knocked on it. "Sir? I am finished with these two and am ready for a few more."

Tnasha listened, but no answer came. After a moment, she grabbed the lantern hanging from the long hook that hung from one of the rafters and carried it over to the area of books from where librarian had pulled the other two books. If she was stuck here for a while, she might as well keep searching. She ran her fingers down their dusty spines, but none of them seemed to be about magick at all. Many of them appeared to be boring philosophical and elemental treatises. Moving through the stacks, she couldn't find a single book about magick. Maybe she'd just missed them.

She went back to the door, this time banging on it loudly with her fist. "Librarian, Sir?" she yelled. Then she hung the lantern back on the hook and went back to the first book. "One doesn't lock a sorceress in a rare book room and then leave her there," she growled under her breath. She flipped through the pages until she found it: a very basic unlock spell.

Sure, she could have threatened to burn the books, but the librarian would know better. No sorcerer worth his or her salt would destroy knowledge, sacred or not. Then she half-laughed at herself. Perhaps the librarian couldn't hear her or had left to go get breakfast. A nagging feeling in the pit of her stomach told her otherwise. With the lack of books about magick in the stacks, she had to wonder if she hadn't been locked in on purpose. But why? And who, besides Aithian and her father, knew she was here anyway? She hadn't told anyone. There were spies and seers as she well knew but locking her in a vault no more assured the sorcerers' victory than it damned them. One hundred or more sorcerers were still more powerful together than two sorcerers - or a single sorceress on her own.

After repeating the spell under her breath a few times, she got up and went to the door. "Upon this door, thrice I knock, turn the handle, spring the lock," she whispered at the door. Then she lightly rapped on the thick wood with one hand, while the other sat on the knob. All the while she imagined its inner workings unlocking and springing open. There was a click and the handle turned. She opened it and looked into the hallway. There was no one there.

This trip had been futile and taken valuable hours of her time. She had to get back to the castle and the meeting where Aithian and the other sorcerers were making two plans. One that included Seth and Alax with weapons, and one where they were without.

She didn't bother closing the door or putting out the lanterns. Carefully, she made her way through the corridor back into the library. As she emerged into the much brighter outer chamber, she saw the librarian, leading Graneck straight toward her.

Lovely, she thought. One never knew who was working with whom or what their motives were.

"Did you break my door?" The librarian rushed past, wide-eyed, his keys jingling.

Tnasha shook her head and looked at Graneck. "Is he always so paranoid, or just when he works with you?"

"I asked him long ago to call me if you ever came to the library."

"Yes, well you could have just invited me for tea. His rare books on magick were about as useful as teats on a male hog." She fought the urge to cross her arms over her chest. Trying to bring the priest over to her side, or to at least give her a chance, seemed a better option than outright snubbing him with defiance.

Graneck glared at her. "Crass."

"Now you sound like Seth and Alax. Last time I checked, no one in this room worshiped an unnamed god who found teats on a male hog offensive." She managed a smile, knowing it looked as forced as it felt.

"You need to allow the men to deal with Alax and Seth. Then, were I you, I would find a new country to live in. Perhaps you could disappear with your friends, back to Arkeereon." Graneck looked past her to the librarian who had come back from the vault.

The little man gave her a stern look. "Everything is fine in there," he said before disappearing back into the stacks.

"You won't be satisfied if I just leave," Tnasha continued. "I know you think I'm an abomination who should be destroyed. I'm not imbecilic." She started toward the door, but the priest's hand shot out and grabbed her by the elbow.

"Perhaps in a fight against Seth and Alax, I'll get my wish, then. We could do with fewer dangerous sorcerers in the world." His eyes glittered coldly above a sinister smile. "It's a shame you don't have any books on magick to draw from."

With an exaggerated snort, she huffed from the room, letting the anger burn inside her all the way back to the castle.

***

She found Aithian and the other sorcerers sitting in the great dining hall, several of them with their feet up on the table. For an instant, Tnasha imagined what her mother would do say if she discovered them like that. The room went quiet when she entered.

"Gentlemen." She looked at Aithian and shook her head.

The skin around his eyes tightened ever so slightly, but he straightened in his chair, smiling brightly, and clapped his hands for attention. "Men! We must move forward in dealing with the magical weapons directly. But with so many of us, that shouldn't be a problem."

Tnasha felt her own spirits rise in response. As always, Aithian amazed her with how collected he seemed to be.

Each of the Angorans present had at least ten to fifteen other sorcerers under him. Without the females, aside from Tnasha, they numbered about one hundred.

"Why doesn't the sorceress just create her own spell? She clearly has the ability to do it," one of the Angorans asked.

All eyes were on her now. Hopeful men with high expectations looked up at her wanting an answer. She thought back to the unlock spell that she used on the door to the rare book vault. Spells often employed rhyming as a way for the sorcerer to remember them. It also helped with focus. The Angoran sorcerer had a point. Why couldn't she create her own spell? Of course, if she was going to do that, she would have to do it quickly, and she'd need to test the spell several times just to make sure it worked. There was no room for error.

She'd never written her own spells before. Finally, she said, "I can try it, and we can test it out to make sure it works, but I can't guarantee anything. So, we need to know exactly what we're going to do if we need to confront Seth and Alax and their magical weapon." She paused and squared her shoulders, determined to discuss the last of it. "I imagine Aithian has also discussed with you the fact that we won't be able to leave Seth and Alax alive."

Another Angoran, the one they called Jarn, who had gold cat-like eyes, nodded. "I think that goes without saying. We took away their magickal weapons once, and here we are again. If we let them live they'll continue to do this over and over. We cannot afford to lose any more of our dying race. This is why it's important that we all work together and spend what time we have left, before the Kersians get here, perfecting and practicing as much as we can without exhausting ourselves. We need to go into this battle well-rested, with sharp minds. Especially if we don't want to see anyone on our side get hurt."

Aithian smiled, nodded at the man, and said, "I think we should name you as captain of our sorcerer strike force." Surprise rippled over the face of those present, and they looked to Aithian for further explanation. "What did you think? Tnasha has a lot of gifts, but her mission will be to get the weapon away from them. She might work best with me on that. And all of you will best work with Jarn." He motioned to the Angoran.

Another Angoran nodded in agreement. "Yes, Jarn will be a good captain, and this is a good plan. She needs to concentrate on the spell, and she needs someone to help her do this, and the rest of us – we're the ones who need to worry about shielding the city from the magical weapon if necessary. We can also help take down the Kersian sorcerers. It's not going to be easy, but I think we need to get to it instead of sitting here talking all day. We have no way of knowing how far out the Kersians are. They could arrive at any time, and we need to be ready."

Aithian stood and took a few steps toward Tnasha. "Agreed. The second we get any word of the location of the Kersian forces, you will be informed. The sorcerers have been given the western training field, out past the stables, to work in. I'll send a messenger if we hear anything."

The rest of the men stood, and still optimistic about their chances, they all left, leaving Aithian and Tnasha alone in the great hall.

"I find it hard to believe a temple that size has no books on magick," he said plainly.

"Yes, I would agree with you. I highly suspect Graneck had all of the books removed. His librarian was instructed to notify him if I ever went into the library. The librarian locked me in the rare book vault." She frowned and sat down heavily in one of the wooden chairs.

"He did what?" Aithian's eyes blazed with fury, and all his calm from moments before vanished. "I swear if he touched you... How did you get out?"

She gave him a sly smile. "Unlock spell. Luckily there was one in there with me. They had two very basic books of magick just sitting there that the librarian used as bait to pacify me while he was off notifying Graneck of my activities."

"I'll deal with him later," Aithian said, sitting back down. "We have the spell to contend with first."

Tnasha nodded. Aithian had more than just this encounter to get Graneck back for. There was that incident in Arkeereon, where the sorcerer-priest sent a spell to knock Aithian out. Aithian had decided to put her welfare over his own anger, or he was holding a grudge and quietly planning revenge. Or both. She couldn't tell and she didn't want to ask.

Finally, she said, "Yes, I was thinking about that when the Jarn mentioned it. Most spells rhyme so that the mage remembers them, and the repetitious sounds facilitate concentration and focus. It's the concentration and focus on the willpower that works, not the magick words. This may be why my spells have been failing so much. I haven't actually connected with the words on previous attempts. I never considered that I could write my own, but it makes sense. I still remember the lock spell." She closed her eyes and recited it from memory. "Upon this door, thrice I knock, turn the handle, spring the lock. I knocked three times, I imagined the lock opening, and I when turned the door handle, it was unlocked."

"Well, it doesn't sound so hard." Aithian raised an eyebrow, then shrugged. "I wonder why there so many books about magick if it's really that simple."

"Well, maybe it isn't," she said. That would've been her luck, but she hoped that her luck was changing. "We'll have to try it and find out."

"I'll go grab some parchment and a quill," he said, jumping up.

"Try the castle library," she told him. While he was gone she started trying to think of words that rhymed with weapon. There wasn't a lot of them, but then it hit her. It wasn't a perfect rhyme, but it might do. "Through an open portal, I draw and beckon, away from them, the magick weapon."

She silently whispered this over and over to herself until Aithian finally returned with a piece of parchment, a quill, and a bottle of ink. She wrote the rhyme down quickly, then blew on the black ink, coaxing it to dry. Once she was satisfied the ink wouldn't smear, she handed it to Aithian. "What do you think?"

He read it silently, then nodded and looked at her. "It should work, maybe. We'll just have to test it. But how are you going to open the portal?"

Now she had to think of a spell to open the portal using the Eagle's Talon to do it. She'd done before, but it had been messy and confusing, and she really didn't know how she'd done it. A muscle under her left eye twitched and she felt a sudden, sharp pain in the back of her head. Another headache, likely induced by anxiety. "Focus, focus," she said to herself.

Very little rhymed with portal. Aithian gaze weighed heavily on her, distracting her from the words she needed. "I can't think with you looking at me."

He laughed. "Is there anything I can help with?"

"I can't think of anything that rhymes with portal," she said, her voice on the verge of panic. The first one had come so easily, but with the portal... Perhaps this is why magicians needed more advanced, more archaic texts: because rhyming wasn't nearly as easy as one would think.

She could almost see Aithian's mind race, looking for a word that rhymed with portal. His facial expression suggested he was having no luck. "Does it have to rhyme?"

"It will be easier for me to remember and not mess it up if it does," she said.

"What about aural," Aithian asked.

"What does that mean?" Tnasha was well read, but their languages had so many words it was impossible to know all of them.

"It has to do with the sense of hearing." He shrugged.

With a sigh, she leaned back. There was no way a word about hearing could be used in a spell about a portal. Closing her eyes, she tried to put the words together in some meaningful way. Meaning was important: it helped with focus. She concentrated on the Eagle's Talon. She wished it were here with her instead of up in her chambers.

Something about staring into the gray stone relaxed her. She imagined it glowing. In her mind's eye, she looked into the stone. The stone looked back.

She heard Aithian jump up, and her eyes flew open. He practically knocked the chair over. He pointed to the Eagle's Talon now laying atop the table. "How did that get here?"

"For a sorcerer, you sure are skittish around sorcery," she admonished.

He seemed to visibly relax, but not without effort, even if it was just to save face.

"The staff and I, we have this sort of mind link." She reached out and grabbed it, pulling it to her, letting her hand caress the smooth eye of the stone. "I was wishing it was here with me so I could look into it to see if it could inspire any ideas about the spell. And it came to me."

She was both in awe and mystified by the staff and her own power. Maybe Graneck was right to be afraid of her. Maybe she should have been more afraid of herself. But she knew herself and trusted herself enough to know that she was only dangerous when backed into a corner. Just like any animal.

"At least it was you who summoned it," he said, settling back into his chair.

She looked into the stone and let her sight go far beyond it. The reflections in the stone faded, and beyond the fade, she saw a myrtle plant with crepe blossoms colored bright pink. The connection came to her a heartbeat later. Myrtle – portal. She remembered from her training with Kalath that myrtle was often used in both love magick and protection. Protection seemed the more likely usage in this instance. She opened her eyes and leaned over the parchment again and wrote down three myrtle blossoms as an ingredient to the spell. Luckily the myrtle was in bloom right now, and there was plenty of it in the garden.

"For protection now, and to the gods, I offer thee this myrtle, this water, too, a drop of blood, to open up this portal." Tnasha wrote this down furiously, adding to the ingredients of the spell water and a drop of blood. When she was finished, she pushed the page over to Aithian, so he could read it.

He nodded. "Now we just have to try it. You were able to retrieve the staff from your chambers, so maybe you don't need a spell."

"But I think the staff is connected to me, and that's why it shows up everywhere I go, or does my bidding even without me realizing it. We have a connection. I can feel it." She pulled the piece of parchment from him and blew on it until the ink was dry. "These will work. Maybe I should write a spell book. That way, after I'm dead, a sorcerer in the future will have a working book of spells."

"You should," Aithian said. "And if you don't mind, please don't tell anyone that the staff appearing like that made me jump."

Tnasha laughed. "I won't tell anyone, but I will tease you mercilessly until our dying day."

"You little brat!" He playfully swiped at her arm.

"I'm sure I will do more to make you jump as the years go on." She gave him a flirtatious smile, then picked up the parchment with her spells carefully written out and started toward the door. "Come on. We have to find something that I can transport through an open portal."

Aithian followed with enthusiasm.

CHAPTER 29

She sat in her room, cross-legged on the carpet holding the Eagle's Talon in her hand. Somewhere in the library of the castle, two long sticks had been hidden from her, and it was now her job to find them. She gazed into the gray orb of the Eagle's Talon, watching the swirls of gray light move through it. In her mind's eye, she felt the staff connect with her. She reached out and dropped three myrtle blossoms into a bowl in front of her, then poured a cup of water over the blossoms. Next, she took a sewing needle and pricked her thumb, allowing a single drop of blood to fall from her finger into the bowl. She recited the spell. "For protection now, and to the gods, I offer thee this myrtle, this water, too, a drop of blood, to open up this portal."

In front of her, the air began to shimmer, displacing the air, and the wall in front of her vanished. Distorted images of the library entered her mind as the portal opened. She immediately closed her eyes and recited the second spell, which originally went: *Through open portal, I draw and beckon, away from them, the magick weapon.* But for the purpose of the experiment, she modified it to retrieve the sticks. "Through open portal, I draw betwixt, away from them, a plain old stick."

She felt a whoosh of air, then heard something clatter to the floor in front of her. Her eyes flew open. There, on the wood floor just beyond the carpet, lay a single, unremarkable stick. With a smile, she repeated both spells a second time. A second stick came through.

176

Aithian ran into the room a few minutes later, out of breath. "It worked?" His eyes traveled to the sticks in front of her, and a wide grin made its way across his face.

"Yes. Now the obvious problem…" She bit her lower lip as her eyes met his.

Aithian's face fell. "What?"

"I'm going to have to know the general location of the weapon or weapons if there is more than one." She paused, gauging his reaction. "I'm going to have to get close enough to where I can at least *see* the encampment."

He absently scratched the back of his head. "Let's try some different locations and figure out just how close *we're* going to have to get."

Warmth filled her chest, and she smiled at him. "All right."

They did it again, but this time, Aithian hid the sticks in an undisclosed location. This time, she didn't use more myrtle, water, and blood. She used what already sat in front of her. Like the time before, the recitation of the spell brought with it the shimmer in the air, vanishing walls, and distorted images. However, this time, nothing came through.

The third time, they tried it with the sticks hidden in the stable. She knew where they were this time. Like the last, she didn't repeat the part with the myrtle, water, and blood. The third time - it worked. The sticks clattered to the floor, one by one, with the recitation of the spell.

She let out an exasperated sigh when Aithian returned. "There's no way getting around this. I have to know the general location in order to find the item and bring it through."

Aithian sat down on the floor next to her and put a strong arm around her shoulders, drawing her to him in a half-embrace. "I suppose that makes sense. Isn't that the way it works with portals?"

"Yes." She looked up at him, somber and tired. "The person opening the portal needs to know where they're going in order to open it to the right location."

"Don't worry." He hugged her to him and kissed the top of her head. "Do you want to try it again? Just two more times. Once where you know the general location of where they are, and again not knowing."

Tnasha gave him a weak smile. "Yes. We probably should."

He tipped her chin toward him and looked deep into her eyes. "Even if you have to get close, I'll be there with you. We may have to get near the camp under cover of darkness in order to do it."

"I may have to repeat the spell more than once. I have no idea how many magickal weapons they have. I just saw the one in my vision, and it was big." A chill of dread ran through her, and she shivered.

Aithian rubbed her arm. "I know."

"On the bright side," she said, forcing a smile. "…it does seem to work with only three myrtle blossoms, one cup of water, and a drop of blood. That part of the spell does not require repetition."

Aithian chuckled and kissed her again. "Your fingers will be grateful for that," he said.

***

The news of the Kersians' location came in while they were eating the evening meal.

"Sire," the sentry addressed the King. After a long day of preparation and training, the King dined among his military leaders and sorcerers in the great hall. Representatives of the temple had come, too. Priestess Caitlan, as usual, and, of course, Graneck.

When the Sentry was sure he had the King's attention, he said, "We have discovered the Kersians in the hills just north of here. They're camped in the foothills of the Onyx mountains."

Tnasha set her fork down in a moment of melancholy. Memories of Kalath and the last incident on the northern fortification of the city came back to Tnasha. Of course, they would have chosen that side to come in on. It offered the most protection and more places to hide a large army.

"Are you sure they haven't broken off into more than one group to surround us?" the King, Tnasha's grandfather, asked.

"Yes, Sire. We have scouts covering all of the borders, and that is where they found them."

"Then tonight would be a good night to do this and get it over with," the King said, looking at Tnasha with weary eyes. "They will likely bolt once they realize their magickal weapons are gone. Unless we want to let it go one more day, which will put them at a close enough distance to the Northern fortification to use their weapons."

General Kale nodded. "I agree, Sire. It will have to be done tonight." Kale looked around the table at the sorcerers and command staff, who were all in good spirits. "Are our troops and sorcerers well-rested? Or will the sorcerers require rest after a day of practice? I know the practice of magick tires them."

Tnasha didn't feel tired at all. In fact, she felt elated. Excited even, that her magick could work.

"Excuse me," Graneck said, setting his ale back on the table. "I take it a spell was found that could remove the weapons from the Kersian sorcerers' possession?"

Graneck stared at her as if surprised. *I bet he is,* Tnasha thought. After all, he'd removed all the books that could have helped her from the library.

"You could say that," Aithian said.

"May I ask…" Graneck began.

Aithian cut Graneck off. "No. That's a secret to remain among the sorcerers. We're not even using Tnasha to do it. We have a secret weapon of our own. A more powerful sorcerer who already knows how to do this. One of the Angorans. Even we didn't know of his existence until today."

Graneck's eyes widened, and a scowl made its way across his face. "I'm a sorcerer, and I demand…"

Aithian shook his head. "No," he repeated.

In the brief time he'd known many of them, Aithian had gained the trust of the soldiers around the table, and Tnasha was pleased to see them readily go along with the lie.

"Yes," one of the Angorans said. "Armand is a deadly force to be reckoned with, but if we had told any of you, Priest Graneck would have wanted him murdered."

General Kale exchanged a look with the King, and the King said, "Yes. See Graneck – there is a solution to every problem. You think my granddaughter an abomination, but there are others like her, and if you notice – the world, and all of us, are still here. Let's count ourselves lucky that the Kersian sorcerers aren't blessed with the same mana that terrifies you so much."

"I have offended all of you and I know when I'm not wanted. I will take my leave." Graneck stood, threw his cloth napkin on the table, tipped his head at Caitlan with a frown, and strode from the room.

The King fought back a grin. "If I had known that's all it would have taken to rid ourselves of Priest Graneck, I would have said something like that long ago." He took a drink from the cup of wine in front of him, set it down, and addressed everyone present. "Now that he's gone, is there anyone else opposed to the plan of Armand? And have we established yet if the troops are ready?"

Everyone, except maybe Caitlan and a few of the commanders, knew that Armand didn't exist.

"Well, I'm ready," Tnasha said, leaning back in her chair. Her belly was full.

Aithian looked at the sorcerers' newly appointed captain, Jarn, who gave him a nod from across the table. "The sorcerers are ready. We'll have one of the Angoran sorcerers start transport of the troops and sorcerers, using this scout's memory, to the site where the Kersian camp was seen, and then we'll get the weapons." Tnasha noticed he was sure not to say her name in case Graneck had spies here, too. Aithian continued. "The sorcerers will disable the Kersian sorcerers using a netting spell they worked on today, or a shield and netting if for some reason we're unable to retrieve the weapons. Once the sorcerers are disabled, General Kale's troops will move in to deal with the human army. We'll save the deed of putting down the Kersian sorcerers to the last possible minute."

Tnasha stared into her cup of burgundy wine, wondering what Morvack would say if he knew about their plan to dispose of his brothers. Would he have begged for their lives? Would he grieve for them? She and Aithian had decided earlier in the day that not telling Morvack anything and keeping him out of harm's way, sequestered in safety with the elder sorcerers of Arkeereon, was the kindest way to deal with the situation. Then, once they confirmed that Seth and Alax were dead, they would inform Natyis and let him break the news to Morvack, who could then grieve as he saw fit. Morvack would now be the last of his bloodline.

Aithian touched her hand, pulling her out of her thoughts. "Are you all right?"

She gave him a sad smile. "I'm fine. I'm just a little tired."

With a nod, Aithian drew his hand back and reached for his ale. "Perhaps you should take a brief nap before we head out?"

"I should," she agreed, forcing a broader smile. Secretly, her stomach was in knots. Maybe she should lie down, if only to clear her head. *Focus on the weapons and nothing else,* she thought. With that, she stood and excused herself.

CHAPTER 30

Seth removed the two hand-held magical weapons from the black felt bags they were stored in and handed one to Alax. during their journey here, the two of them had spent a good deal of time going over the methods of warding the camp against magick. Seth had thought of everything.

"We do it just like we discussed," Seth told Alax. "Remember the words and the type of energy to put through the scepter."

"Yes, I recall very well," Alax said, his voice far away. There was a tone to it that made Seth uneasy. It wasn't arrogance or annoyance or even boredom. That would have been normal for Alax. Instead, it sounded like resignation.

"We're going to win this, you'll see," Seth told him, forcing an encouraging smile. But even to him, it felt fake.

"Indeed." Alax moved off to the north side of the camp and began erecting walls of protective energy. The fluidity and ease with which he did it made Seth smile. At least something still came easily for his brother.

Then Seth turned to his own quadrants and began doing the same thing, enjoying the power that flowed through him and through the scepter, building a wall of magick surrounding the entire camp. It took longer to complete than he'd anticipated, but when they were finished, they met at the larger weapon and had it moved to the edge of the camp facing Danaria. Just like they had in Arkeereon, they would blast through the battlements and send the entire city up in flames.

Seth's daydreaming revelry ended as a shadowy figure approached the edge of the camp, arms lifted in surrender. Finally, the priest. Gavgal had worked with the Danarian priest off and on for years, and after Gavgal's death, Seth had taken meetings with the suspicious man more than once, but only because he'd proven himself a useful informant. Now, Seth smiled, hoping the priest had news of Danaria's plan of attack and defense.

"Graneck," Seth greeted. Alax hovered quietly behind him. The soldiers patted down the aging priest. Once they were sure he carried no weapons, they allowed him to pass.

"Seth. It is good to see you're well." Graneck gave him a sneer rather than a smile.

Seth nodded once. "Yes, but you did not come by to see to my health. What news do you have?"

"That meddlesome sorceress has plans to take your weapons by magical means, though I doubt she could do it. The girl is dangerous, even to herself. I've also hidden all of the grimoires in the temple from her." Graneck looked around as if inspecting the Kersian camp. "I sincerely hope you can accomplish what your brother failed to do."

Seth felt his frown deepen. "I thought I had. She was as good as dead last I saw her."

"Yes, well, she has a nasty habit of not dying." Graneck narrowed his eyes. "See to it that you make no mistakes this time."

"Last time I checked, you weren't my emperor, though I am yours. Guards." Seth motioned to his guards, who rushed to Graneck's side, restraining him.

Graneck lifted his chin haughtily. "You do realize I *am* a sorcerer."

"Hmm." Alax stepped forward, set his scepter against the priest's chest, and pushed a single pulse of mana through the weapon, instantly knocking the man unconscious.

"What was that for?" Seth asked, a large grin covering his face.

"His prattling was annoying. Get him out of the way. We don't have time for his nonsense. Our protective wards should keep the sorceress from getting our weapons," Alax said, frowning.

Seth laughed, amused by his brother's annoyance. "Yes, do as the *Grand Mage* says." The soldiers scurried to do his bidding.

CHAPTER 31

Preparation took almost two hours. Tnasha carried a satchel with the myrtle, a canister of water, and put a needle through the sleeve of her shirt. She also carried a dagger, a short sword, and of course the Eagle's Talon.

The Angorans had perfected portal travel from one place to another. It was how their tribes could remain so elusive in the deep forests of the Onyx Mountains. It took over an hour for three Angorans to transport one hundred sorcerers and over two hundred soldiers. Now, the sorcerers and soldiers fanned out, surrounding the tents and burning fires of the Kersian encampment from a distance.

Tnasha kneeled behind an outcropping of rock and started the spell. Just like at the castle, she dropped three Myrtle blossoms into a bowl in front of her, then poured some water from the flask over the blossoms. Then she took the sewing needle from her sleeve and pricked her thumb, allowing a single drop of blood fall from her finger into the bowl. She recited the spell. "For protection now, and to the gods, I offer thee this Myrtle. This water, too, a drop of blood, to open up this portal."

In front of her... nothing. Then she felt it. A solid wall. The Kersians, or more appropriately Seth and Alax, had erected protective wards around their campsite.

"What's wrong?" Aithian asked. A look of panic flashed through his eyes.

"They put up wards." She took a deep breath.

"What do we do?" he whispered.

"Don't panic and tell no one anything yet. I wrote spells to do this. I can create spells to take down their protective barriers." She looked into the Eagle's Talon and the stone glowed eerily back at her. Inside it, she saw the gray curling smoke. It cleared, and the spell revealed itself to her. "I pray to Ba'al for his direction, to help destroy this ward protection!"

She felt something pull from within her and swoop outward, and then she was overcome by a cold sensation, like melted snow, that washed over her unbidden. The wall was down.

She whispered to Aithian, "They may have warded the weapons, too."

He nodded. The look on his face was that of concern, but she didn't have time to reassure him now.

Again, she tried the open portal spell. "For protection now, and to the gods, I offer thee this myrtle. This water, too, a drop of blood, to open up this portal."

A rush of joy ran through her as the air began to displace, and the rock in front of her disappeared. Her vision distorted, and the portal opened. She kept her eyes open and recited the second spell: "Through open portal, I draw and beckon, away from them, the magick weapon."

Nothing. All right, she told herself inwardly. You can do this, Tnasha. Just create a spell to release all protections and bindings from the weapons.

"Don't panic," she told Aithian. "I'm almost there."

One of the commanders rushed to Aithian's side. He crouched low and whispered something into Aithian's ear.

"She's having to remove some protections. One down, and one to go," he said. By the tone of the whisper, Tnasha could tell he wasn't so sure.

She nodded at him. Again, she looked deep into the stone of the Eagle's Talon, vaguely aware of the sweat droplets forming on her forehead. The words fell from her lips strained and deep, as if she was possessed by divine intelligence. "Break, unbind all the Kersians spells, and leave them barren where they dwell. Unbind their spells, destroy their weapons, that I may bring them as I beckon."

Cringing, she opened her eyes and wiped the sweat from her brow. *That one was a little clunky,* she thought. Not nearly as pretty as the rest of them. But she hoped it was enough to work.

Her knees had gone weak, but she gathered her strength in a deep cleansing breath. Then she redid the spell to pull the magick weapons from the Kersian camp. "Through open portal, I draw and beckon, away from them, the magick weapon."

Her stomach turned violently, and she tasted the bile in her throat. She spat up the foul liquid and forced her attention back to her intent. In front of her, the first one appeared. She repeated the spell. A second weapon came through. The third time, there was a thunderous thunk as the large weapon, the one attached to a cart, came to rest barely a foot in front of her. The fourth time, nothing came through, and she vomited and clutched at the rock. Her head spun and throbbed. It took her a few minutes to regain her bearings. There had only been three weapons with no more left. But scarcely had she finished the final spell when the Kersian camp guards sounded the alarm in a series of shouts.

Aithian took her by the arm to steady her and nodded at the commander. "Go!"

Then, scooping up both weapons, Tnasha handed them off to the waiting Angoran portal-walkers who disappeared with them in bright flashes of light. The carted weapon would have to stay where it was and be dismantled and destroyed later. Hopefully, Seth or Alax would not find it here.

Tnasha picked up the Eagle's Talon as Aithian helped her to her feet. "Will you be all right?"

She nodded and drew in another deep breath. "Yes. Let's go."

Together, she and Aithian made their way toward the encampment.

Her heart pounded wildly in her chest. The battle had already started. Before them, steel ripped into steel and flesh in a fierce cacophony of battle cries. Aithian grabbed her hand and held on, practically dragging her through a maze of melee and fallen bodies. Her mind began clearing, the effects of such intense sorcery waning, though her legs still felt weak and her stomach still sour.

Sheer willpower forced her forward. She knew she had to be there for the final blows that would end Seth and Alax. It wasn't something she wanted to do, but she had to make sure this couldn't happen again. Had to make sure they were dead. Too many people had died needlessly already.

Fear gripped her stomach, but she went boldly forward, letting out her mana, allowing it bloom into full light, illuminating the darkness around them. Her mana was her shield, the Eagle's Talon her weapon. She would never be a victim.

Eyes blazing, she and Aithian managed to find themselves at the center of the Kersian camp, its tents bathed in orange shadows cast by the firelight. She stopped and pulled her hand from Aithian's and looked around. The sounds of fighting were more subdued and distant now. The Sirus Horde had done their jobs well, without the help of sorcery. At swordpoint, manacled and resigned Kersion lined up on command - prisoners of war. With their faces tired and their clothing dirty, many of them seemed almost glad to be taken away.

To her right, twenty Angoran sorcerers had used their magical nets and wrangled both Seth and Alax to the ground. She started toward them.

Aithian grabbed her elbow. "Let them do it."

"No." She towered over the Kersian sorcerers and looked down on them. Any anger she had for them had been replaced with pity. They looked so helpless, harmless. Without their enchanted weapons and legions of soldiers, these men, these sorcerers, were both magically impotent.

The golden light of the nets gleamed up at her, like lighted spider webs. Beneath them, Seth and Alax were trapped, unable to struggle or move, their eyes wide with fear. They knew this was it.

Tnasha let out a sad sigh. "Do either of you have anything to say?"

Aithian stepped closer to her. "Tnasha…"

"No," she gave him a cold, sideways glance. "Let them speak."

"I'll see you in hell, wench," Seth spat.

Even that did not stir her anger. Her eyes turned to Alax.

Alax closed his eyes and his facial muscles visibly relaxed. The fear vanished. "Do it."

Seth's eyes turned toward his brother, wide, angry. His muscles tensed as he tried to break free. "Use sorcery to block it, break the net!"

Laughter tumbled from Alax's throat. "You never gave me time to read the books, so I could learn that. Face it, Seth, your hunger for power has killed us all. I'll finally be free of you."

Seth's face contorted from anger to fear, and he howled.

Aithian gave her a knowing look and stood back. They both knew what she had to do.

Tnasha lifted the Eagle's Talon. It had to be quick because she couldn't bear to see them suffer no matter how horrendous and evil she found their deeds. She drew in a breath. One blate each would kill them, but blate burns could be painful and cause unnecessary suffering.

For the final time that night she looked into the stone of the Eagle's Talon, past the swirling smoke and into the fade. The spell came gently and rang in her ears. She looked at Seth first, deep into his wide, terrified eyes. "For your crimes on our kind, ever die you must. A gentle breath, your body's last, shall all be turned to dust."

Like an explosion of golden sand, Seth's body melted before their eyes and turned to nothing.

Suddenly, Alax screamed in horror. Then he began to beg. "Please, no, I was only…"

"Shhh. It will be quick and painless, I promise." And this silenced him. He squeezed his eyes shut and drew in a deep breath, but she looked upon him anyway. She repeated the spell, and with another shimmer of gold sand, it was over. The Angoran sorcerers allowed their magick net to dissipate into the ether, and left Tnasha standing there, looking at the piles of dust that had been Seth and Alax.

She felt a firm arm go around her shoulders. "Tnasha," Aithian whispered. "It's over. Come on."

He led her back toward the waiting Angoran portal-walkers who had returned to take them all home.

Most of the Kersian soldiers resigned themselves to shackles and cooperated. Several did not and had to be wrestled to the ground.

But one, one refused to go down quietly to allow the soldiers to shackle him.

"Unhand me!" The voice was familiar.

Tnasha started toward them as did General Kale and two commanders. It took four men to finally wrestle the fighting man to the ground and shackle him. Then they lifted him to his feet, turning him toward the groups of prisoners awaiting transport to the castle dungeons where they would await their fate by the High Council. When the light hit the man's face, Tnasha gasped. There stood Graneck, wild-eyed and mortified to find himself a prisoner – of his own people.

"Well, well, well," said General Kale. "We suspected you were up to something underhanded, we just weren't sure what."

"That's why they put up the wards and put protections on the weapons," she said aloud. "You warned them. You bastard!"

"I did no such thing! They figured out the wards on their own. I was here to fight," he said in protest.

"You were unconscious on the ground when I got here," one of the soldiers said.

Tnasha started toward him with the Eagle's Talon, half-tempted to use the same spell she'd used on Seth and Alax.

Aithian's strong arm caught her and held her back. "He's not worth it. Let the high council and the King deal with him."

The soldiers dragged Graneck, screaming all the way, to stand along with the waiting prisoners.

Kale turned to Tnasha. "This was the easiest raid I've ever seen."

Aithian looked at him with raised eyebrows. "Really?"

"Every last one of their weapons was broken. They had nothing but their hands to defend themselves, and they were outnumbered and out-armed. What kind of crazy emperor brings an ill-prepared army to take down a city as large as ours?" Kale shook his head.

"A crazy sorcerer who thinks he's going to use a magick weapon?" offered one of the commanders half-jokingly.

Kale nodded. "I suppose so. It's time to get back." The General ushered them to the front of the line so they could pass through the portal ahead of the prisoners. Another thing for which Tnasha found herself grateful.

Aithian took Tnasha by the elbow and led her toward the portals the Angoran sorcerers were ushering everyone through. He leaned over. "The weapons were all broken?"

She cringed a little inwardly, having hoped no one would suspect her. "I think I may have messed that spell up just a little. But thankfully to our benefit."

He laughed. "Yes, you did."

"I'm just glad I didn't have to do that alone...."

He put his arm around her. "You never have to do it alone, Tnasha," he said. "You've never been alone, not really. All of us, the Angorans, your fellow soldiers, your family, the Arkeeronish – we've all had your back the entire time."

"Have you?"

His eyes widened. "Yes, I think we have."

"Maybe you're right. Maybe I've been so busy playing the martyr I didn't see it." She looked up at the night sky.

With a sheepish grin he looked down at his feet. "Okay, so maybe there have been a few people against you, or worried about you. The point is, you don't have to do it alone ever again."

She nodded but said nothing.

"Tonight, you did something many of us wouldn't have been able to do," he said, quietly. "It was courageous."

She wasn't sure how courageous it was to have killed two madmen who were held down with magickal netting. With a forlorn sigh, she allowed him to lead her through the portal to home.

CHAPTER 32

The Eagle's Talon was gone. Vanished right from her room. Her stomach seethed with anger, wondering who would take it.

"Of course, someone took it," Aithian reasoned with her. "You should have locked it up. It's a magickal item and there are a lot of sorcerers around. Any one of them could have taken it."

When he left to meet his family for the mid-day meal, she stayed behind in her chambers, staring at the empty space where the staff had been. She was just about to perform the spell to bring the staff back to her when there was a knock on her door.

"Who is it?" Annoyance filled her voice.

"A message for you, my lady," came the voice from the other side of the door.

She opened the door and took the folded slip of paper from the soldier, who promptly left after delivering it.

The note was from Priestess Caitlan. After reading it, she decided the staff had to wait. Besides, she had no doubt she could retrieve it from whoever had taken it, and it wouldn't matter how far they were. If anything, the staff had proven to be a faithful companion.

Tnasha couldn't understand why Caitlan wanted to see her. It had been two weeks since the conflict with the Kersians had permanently ended. It was a nice feeling, knowing that things were back to normal. Mostly. Now, her mother, aunts, cousins, and grandmother were busy planning Tnasha's wedding, and Tnasha spent her days hiding out in the training fields or at the stables, Aithian sometimes with her, sometimes not. He'd found plenty to keep himself busy. The Arkeeronish had yet to return to their homeland to rebuild. It was a lot of work for such a small group of people and she was sure they were simply planning before returning home.

The afternoon sky was filled with billowing white and gray clouds that threatened rain. She entered the temple and made her way through long hallways until she arrived at the corridor that led to the great room – a colossal atrium where large rites and gatherings were usually held. Priestess Shanalyn stood outside the doors leading in. The young woman jumped up at the sight of her as if alarmed or surprised.

Tnasha gave her a quizzical look. "Hey, what are you doing here? Are you here to see Priestess Caitlan, too?"

With a secretive smile, Shanalyn knocked on the door to the atrium, waiting for an answer from beyond.

Tnasha shooed her aside and opened the door. The atrium's interior had been decorated for some formal affair. Red and violet banners hung against the walls with garlands of jasmine, lotus, and chrysanthemum strung between them. Inside, the King, the entire high council, the military leaders, the Angoran chieftains, the Arkeeronish elders, the priests and priestesses, and Aithian awaited her.

Ah, another meeting, she thought. But priestesses did not wear their formal, red silk robes to everyday meetings. The General and his commanders wore full military dress too, and the nobles of the council wore their best finery, usually reserved for court. Even the Angorans and Arkeeronish appeared less disheveled and ruffian-like. She entered cautiously, feeling like she had accidentally walked in on something important and was entirely under-dressed. It appeared as though her invitation had been an afterthought.

"Tnasha Adrianna Delepitore Polerissa fen'Schoitt, come forward," Caitlan said, beckoning Tnasha toward her.

She complied, every eye in the room watching her closely. It was all she could do not to wipe her hands on her tunic.

When Tnasha made it to Caitlan's side, another priestess dropped a violet pillow on the floor between them. Now Tnasha was very confused.

"Kneel," Caitlan said.

A surprised look washed over Tnasha's face and she turned from Caitlan to the waiting crowd. Everyone looked so serious, but not in a somber way. It was far more expectant, as if she should have known what was about to happen. Her stomach flipped, and against her better judgement, she kneeled.

"On behalf of all present, and in presence of all the gods, I hereby pronounce you Grand Magus and Royal Mage of Danaria." With that, Caitlan draped a violet ceremonial cape around her shoulders.

Tnasha blinked down in shock at the seal of the magus embroidered in gold thread on the cape's right breast. "You're..." she started.

"Rise," Caitlan said. "All Hail the Grand Magus."

"All Hail!" resounded the voices of those present. Then they began clapping.

Tnasha looked at Aithian who smiled, then at the staff he held. He'd had it all along, waiting for her! When caitlan took the Eagle's Talon from his hands and presented it to Tnasha, the crowd began to applaud again. Tnasha's eyes traveled over everyone present. An overwhelming warmth filled her, like an embrace. From the corner of her eye, and just for a moment, she thought she saw her mentor - the sorcerer Kalath - standing in the crowd, smiling at her.

FINIS

Here ends the final book of the Sorcerers' Twilight trilogy.

ABOUT THE AUTHOR

S. J. Reisner began writing at the age of ten and never stopped. Left Horse Black, the first in her fantasy series, was the product of a thirteen-year daydream. She also writes under the pseudonyms Audrey Brice (urban fantasy, mystery, thriller, horror, paranormal) and Anne O'Connell (erotic romance, paranormal romance).

To learn more visit http://www.sjreisner.com

Left Horse Black

For centuries, the zealot Kersian sorcerers have abducted innocent women and children for sacrifice to their 'no name' god and have waged war upon Danaria's sorcerers. Now, they are covertly usurping the thrones of human-ruled kingdoms to do the unthinkable; they are building a massive human army to assist them in destroying Danaria's sorcerer bloodlines in an attempt to save their own. Armed with nothing more than meager weapons, untrained sorcery, and mere instinct, a troubled human prince, an inept Danarian sorceress, and their friends, rise up and become the world's last hope to stop the Kersians, and save the sorcerers' dying race. Will they succeed?

Other Titles:
Warrior's Blood Red
Saving Sarah May